The Monster of the Month Club Quartet:

Monster of the Month Club
Monsters in the Attic
Monsters in Cyberspace

Forthcoming
Monsters and My One True Love

Happy Holidays
To: Rilla Harmony Earth
Congratulations!
You have received a gift membership
to the *Monster of the Month Club*

January

Icicle

February

Sweetie Pie

March

Shamrock

April

Chelsea

May

Burly

June

Summer

M.O.T.M. Club Rules:

1. A new monster selection arrives on the first day of every month.

2. The monsters come from different countries around the globe.

3. Instructions for the care and feeding of each monster are included in every box.

4. Good luck . . .

IN CYBERSPACE

Dian Curtis Regan
Illustrated by Melissa Sweet

Henry Holt and Company　New York

Henry Holt and Company, Inc.
Publishers since 1866
115 West 18th Street
New York, New York 10011

Henry Holt is a registered
trademark of Henry Holt and Company, Inc.

Published in Canada by Fitzhenry & Whiteside Ltd.,
195 Allstate Parkway, Markham, Ontario L3R 4T8.

Library of Congress Cataloging-in-Publication Data
Regan, Dian Curtis
Monsters in cyberspace / Dian Curtis Regan; illustrations by
Melissa Sweet.
p.   cm.
Companion volume to: Monster of the Month Club and Monsters
in the attic.
Summary: Thirteen-year-old Rilla tries to hide the fact that her
stuffed toy monsters from the Monster of the Month Club are
coming to life, while their use of her Internet account threatens her
online search for her absent father.
[1. Monsters—Fiction. 2. Toys—Fiction. 3. Internet (Computer
network)—Fiction. 4. Computers—Fiction. 5. Fathers and
daughters—Fiction.] I. Sweet, Melissa, ill. II. Title.
PZ7.R25854Mnj 1996 [Fic]—dc21   96-37559

ISBN 0-8050-4677-1
First Edition—1997
Designed by Meredith Baldwin

Printed in the United States of America on acid-free paper. ∞

1 3 5 7 9 10 8 6 4 2

For Donna Bray

—D.C.R.

Contents

MONSTERS
IN CYBERSPACE

1
Waiting for Mr. T.

Rilla Harmony Earth planted herself in the doorway of Harmony House Bed and Breakfast. She would *not* move from this spot until she saw the airport limo turning into the driveway.

Hurry, hurry, hurry became her mantra.

Reason number one for her excitement was the limo's passenger—Mr. Tamerow, her favorite guest at the B & B (owned by her mother, Sparrow Harmony Earth, and her aunt, Poppy Harmony Earth).

Reason number two was what Mr. Tamerow would have in tow. He traveled all over the globe on business and brought her nifty gifts, like a gold-and-silver sarong from New Delhi and sand dollars from a Greek beach on the Mediterranean Sea.

Or he shipped "bargains" to the Earth family—like Sparrow's photocopier from Montreal, or Aunt

Poppy's Backyard Ride-a-Mower, found at a factory closeout sale in Nutbush, Tennessee.

Today Mr. Tamerow was bringing Rilla her own top-of-the-line home computer he'd stumbled across at an estate sale in Nancy, France. Rilla'd had no idea that a city in France was named Nancy.

"Nancy France, Nancy France, Nancy France," she singsonged as she polished the brass EARTH nameplate on the oak door.

Hurry, hurry, hurry.

Her other computer—clunky and old—would remain in the classroom, an area behind the B & B's kitchen where Rilla studied with five other home-schoolers. The computer was hearty enough for the group to pound on, and provided enough memory for Sparrow's bookkeeping records.

"Are you trying to air-condition the entire world?" came a grumbly voice from inside.

Rilla peeked around the door. Sparrow, grasping a cup of ginseng tea in a mug that read *Have a Green Future,* took her place at the antique registration desk to sort receipts and keys after the morning checkout rush.

"I'm waiting for Mr. Tam—"

"Wait by the window. It's cheaper."

Closing the door, Rilla moved to the window. Sparrow had already complained about hot August weather forcing her to run the air conditioner day *and* night. Rilla didn't want to add any more money worries to Sparrow's list. Not when the Earth family had an extra mouth to feed. Of course, no one knew about the extra mouth—except her.

Rilla wound herself inside the window sheers and pressed her forehead to the warm glass. She couldn't believe Sparrow or Aunt Poppy hadn't noticed "dog food" on the grocery receipts or stumbled across the shaggy mutt in the barn.

Taco made a fun addition to her family of felines: Oreo, the mama cat, and her year-old kittens, Pepsi, Dorito, and Milk Dud. Junk-food names were as close as those words ever got to Harmony House, due to Sparrow's philosophy of "Eat healthy or you'll die," as if those who lived on amaranth and hummus foiled the grim reaper.

Thanks to Joshua Banks (Rilla's one true love), Taco got plenty of exercise and sunshine in nearby Willow Park. Taco was their little secret. Rilla liked having secrets with her one true love.

Be-e-e-e-e-p!

"He's here!" Rilla untangled herself from the sheers and dashed outside. Leave it to Mr. Tamerow to lean over the limo driver and blast the horn.

"Rilly!" Mr. T. called, unfolding his long legs from the backseat. He was dressed in his "traveling pants," with pockets up and down each leg, and a colorful hooded shirt that must have come from some exotic place.

Rilla raced across the front lawn. Mr. Tamerow caught her up in a hug, swinging her around, which didn't embarrass her as it usually did because she was so happy to see him. "Did you bring it?" she exclaimed.

"You bet. I even had the power supply converted to American voltage during my stopover in New York. *And* I know how to get the whole thing up and running although the instructions are in French."

The limo driver helped Mr. Tamerow and Rilla carry bags and boxes of computer equipment to the veranda. Rilla opened the door while Mr. T. tipped the driver—after digging through five pockets and pulling out lire, yen, pesetas, and francs before finding good ol' American dollars.

"Welcome, Abe!" Sparrow called, stepping around the registration desk to hug him. "Suite one on the blue floor is free. Sound okay?"

"Free sounds fabulous, mate."

"Oh, uh, I mean, it's *empty,* not free."

Rilla groaned at her mother. "He was *joking.*"

Mr. Tamerow winked.

"I knew that," Sparrow snipped, handing him a key. "Wish you could stay longer than the weekend."

"Me, too," he said.

"Me, three," Rilla added, pretending to pout.

Mr. Tamerow pouted back at her as he shoved his bags beneath the sideboard. "I'll leave these here for now. The important thing is to get this computer up to the attic so Rilly can tune into the globe."

Rilla wasn't sure what he meant, but she was eager to find out.

Hoisting the smaller box, she led Mr. Tamerow up the curved stairway to the green floor (wallpapered with herbs and flowers). Down the hall they paraded, up the steps to the blue floor (splashed with stars and moons), then up the creaky, narrow attic steps to Rilla's room.

Balancing the box on one hip, Rilla unlocked the door with a key she wore on a silver chain around her neck. Inside, she dumped the box onto her waterbed and directed Mr. T. toward the desk, which she'd cleaned off in honor of the new computer.

Mr. Tamerow pulled a Swiss Army knife from one of his pockets and sliced the mailing tape. His gaze traveled the sunny room as he worked. "Any new arrivals in the Monster of the Month Club?"

Rilla's heart went into a tailspin.

Monsters.

Why did that word—coming from a grownup—shake her up like an impending plane crash?

Because, her inner voice reminded her, *grown-ups don't know that monsters in the M.O.T.M. Club aren't "cozy collectibles," as the legend implies.*

Grown-ups don't know the monsters are REAL. And very much alive. . . .

Monsters and Modems

Well, sometimes *the monsters are real and alive,* she reminded her inner voice. *But not today, thank heavens.*

Mr. Tamerow was the one who'd given her the subscription to the Monster of the Month Club, but even *he* didn't know the legend was true.

Raising an eyebrow, Mr. T. questioned her silence.

In answer, Rilla dug through the pile of stuffed animals on her bed to find the newest monsters. The last two had arrived stuffed and silent, the way the M.O.T.M. Club intended them to be.

Rilla imagined Mr. Tamerow's shocked reaction if he'd stepped into her attic to find eight *live* monsters getting into mischief—which is mostly what live monsters did.

"These are Sparkler and Butterscotch, the July and August selections."

Rilla propped the cat-sized monsters against the dresser, then opened the bottom drawer to find the cookie tin which held their monthly selection cards, or birth announcements, as she liked to call them.

Mr. Tamerow yanked packing material from the computer box and dropped it onto the floor. "Read me the legend again."

Rilla drew out the largest card. " 'Legend of the Global Monsters,' " she began. " 'Once, when stranger things than monsters roamed the earth, these tiny creatures shared nature with us, living in small colonies scattered throughout the world. Belief held that spotting a mini-monster in the wild meant good fortune would follow for a year.

" 'Today, likenesses of the monsters have been created as cozy collectibles. Yet, legend warns, when stars line up in angled shapes like lightning, real global monsters tread the earth once more.' "

Mr. Tamerow shot her a mischievous grin as he lifted a computer monitor from the box. "Wouldn't it be *wild* if the legend was true?"

Rilla peered at him. He'd asked the question in a voice that wasn't quite his. He sounded younger, thirteenish—like Joshua Banks or one of the other home-schoolers, Andrew Hogan or Wally Pennington.

Rilla gulped. "The legend *is* true. All legends are. That's what Ms. Noir at the library told me." Rilla inched closer, holding Mr. T.'s gaze as if it might make him realize how serious she was. "Ms. Noir said legends are based on truths. Even truths formed centuries ago."

"Ho, Rilla." Mr. Tamerow chuckled, his voice zapping back to its grown-up baritone. "I envy your youthful fancy."

Rilla's heart pounded. "But it *is* true." She'd been trying to tell him so ever since Icicle, the January selection, had shown up alive and rascally in the Earth mailbox.

Mr. T. was the only grown-up she could trust with her monster secret. *He'd* never take them away, which is what Sparrow would do—send them off to the We Care Animal Shelter, where she'd tried to dump Oreo and her kittens last spring.

Mr. T. cocked his head and squinted at Sparkler and Butterscotch, as though imagining them alive, then gave Rilla an envious smile.

She sighed. *How can he believe me when the monsters are obviously stuffed?* Digging into the cookie tin, she retrieved the July and August selection cards. "Do you want to hear about these two?"

Mr. Tamerow was peering intently at *Les directions pour l'assemblage*. "Definitely," he answered. "Introduce me."

Rilla sat on the floor and picked up the July monster. His fur was striped red, white, and blue, and his ears were long and puppy-doggish. He wore a jean vest, cutoffs, and knee pads. His pockets were filled with tiny, dime-store toys and a small deck of cards. He even came with his own mini-skateboard.

Rilla read his birth announcement:

Monster of the Month Club

July Selection

Name: Sparkler   *Gender:* Male

Homeland: Kowloon, Hong Kong

Likes: Hot dogs, chips, apple pie

Is fond of loud noises.

"Ha," was Mr. Tamerow's response.

Rilla picked up the August monster. She wore a peasant dress and sandals. Embroidered on the yoke of her dress was:

Peace~~Paz~~Paix

The monster wore dangly love beads. Her flowing hair and fuzzy fur matched her name—Butterscotch. The card read:

Monster of the Month Club
August Selection
Name: Butterscotch   *Gender:* Female
Homeland: Kathmandu, Nepal
Likes: Honey, granola, tofu
Shy. Needs lots of peace and quiet.

Rilla glanced up to watch Mr. Tamerow's reaction.

His nose was buried in the assembly booklet, his brows wrinkled in confusion. Cords and cables snaked across Rilla's desk like an electronic octopus.

"Is something wrong?" she asked.

"No, no. Soon as I figure out the instructions, all will be well."

Rilla peeked over his shoulder. "I thought you could speak French."

"Well, I can," Mr. T. began. " '*Bonjour*' is 'Good morning.' '*Parlez-vous anglais?*' is 'Do you speak English?' and '*Où sont les toilettes?*' is . . . well, you can probably figure that one out."

He sighed. "However, I don't know French for 'Install a sturdy surge protector before plugging the serial connector into the modem port.' That's a tricky one."

An hour later, Mr. Tamerow admitted defeat. Calling up a business associate, fluent in French, he asked her to translate the instructions.

What followed was a whirlwind attack of cables and cords, during which Mr. T. looked as though he were being devoured by the octopus. Finally, the computer booted up and began to hum—in English, thanks to new software.

Only then did Mr. Tamerow sprawl on the floor to examine Sparkler and Butterscotch. That's what Rilla loved about him. What other grown-up would sit on the rug and discuss her stuffed animal collection?

Part of her felt silly about it. After all, she was thirteen now—too old for toys. Yet knowing they could spring to life at any moment (according to the legend) made her keep a sharp eye on her fuzzy charges.

Mr. Tamerow gave Sparkler a fatherly pat on the head. "Well, I think it's time to round up my bags, find my suite, and settle in before dinner."

Gathering the empty boxes, he carried them downstairs.

Rilla played with the computer, trying to get used to sliding the mouse around with a minimum of awkward, jerky movements. Mr. Tamerow had bought her a mouse pad with a picture of eight kittens—four real and four stuffed. The irony was not lost on Rilla.

Time to get downstairs and help with dinner. Rilla left the computer humming since Mr. T. said it was okay to leave it on all day.

Before her feet hit the second-floor landing, excited voices met her ears. Sparrow and Aunt Poppy. Were the Earth sisters quarreling? With B & B guests in earshot? How embarrassing.

Below, Sparrow stomped into the foyer. "Rilla Harmony Earth, get down here at once! You just gave your aunt the biggest scare of her life. How did that mangy dog end up in our barn?"

3

Good Dog
Arguments

Oops.

They'd discovered Taco.

Finally.

Slowing, Rilla tried to form a convincing "But we *have* to keep the dog" argument before entering the kitchen.

In June, when Taco showed up with Burly (the May monster) and moved into the barn, Rilla'd had tons of good dog arguments.

Who would've guessed almost three months would pass before Aunt Poppy stumbled across the mutt? Joshua had done a great job of keeping Taco out of sight.

Right now, all Rilla could think was: *Mangy? Taco's not mangy! Joshua gave him a bath in the fountain at Willow Park only a week ago, and I've been brushing him ever since.*

When Rilla got to the kitchen, no one was there. She peeked out the back screen. Sparrow stood on the patio, arms folded in her "Nothing gets past the Earth Mother" stance.

Across the yard, near a mound of upturned earth marking the future site of Sparrow's Home-Grown greenhouse, was long-haired Aunt Poppy, wearing a T-shirt reading *Extinction is Forever.* She loped across the grass, chasing Taco, who yipped happily from all the attention.

"Here she is," Sparrow announced. "Explain, please?"

Aunt Poppy stopped loping. Grabbing Taco's rope collar, she led him to the patio, attempting to replace the grin on her face with a serious frown. "Where'd this guy come from?" she asked. "I nearly jumped out of my skin when he lunged from behind my Ride-a-Mower."

"Taco," Rilla told her. "His name is Taco."

Instantly, she realized offering a name was a mistake. Sparrow still didn't know the cats' names because she didn't believe in naming animals. (It kept them from being all nature intended them to be, according to her.)

Sparrow pursed her lips at the dog the same way

she'd pursed her lips at Oreo, who'd shown up on the veranda last fall, dripping wet, pitiful, and pregnant, although at the time they didn't know about the last part.

"He needed a home," Rilla began.

"We can't give a home to every stray in the neighborhood," Sparrow shot back.

Rilla tried again. "He's really a nice dog." This time, she aimed her comment at Aunt Poppy, who seemed a lot closer to accepting the four-legged guest than Sparrow did.

"And I don't *have* a dog," Rilla added. "You had a dog when you were my age." This was aimed at Sparrow, who had, indeed, told Rilla about her beloved dog, who'd lived for nineteen years.

Sparrow's head tilted side to side, as if arguing Rilla's point to herself. "We'd have to take him to the vet for shots and neutering, and they're expen—"

"Been there; done that." Rilla grinned. She knew she was on the home stretch now. Responsibility was high on Sparrow's list of objectives for the home-schooler curriculum.

"You already took him to the vet?"

"Yes, ma'am."

Approval flickered across Sparrow's face seconds before her eyes narrowed. "How did you pay—?"

"I worked for you all summer, remember?" Rilla left out the part about borrowing money from Joshua Banks to pay the vet bill. (She'd almost finished paying him back, although taking her time meant more face-to-face meetings with her one true love.)

Meanwhile, Aunt Poppy had dropped to her knees to wrestle with Taco and dodge sloppy dog kisses.

Sparrow rolled her eyes skyward. "Against my better judgment, he can stay. As long as he lives in the barn with the cats."

"Done."

Rilla exchanged "all rights" and high fives with Aunt Poppy, then dove into the wrestling match to officially welcome Taco into the Earth family.

She could hardly wait to tell Joshua.

Or should she? If he knew the dog's existence wasn't a secret anymore, he wouldn't have a reason to come to Harmony House—except for classes with the home-schoolers.

Maybe the good news about Taco was best kept a secret—as far as her one true love was concerned.

4

earthgirl

Click . . . hummmm.

The muffled humming of the air conditioner roused Rilla from her almost-awake state. Monday morning. The first day of school. Ugh. How had summer zoomed by so fast?

Stretching, she thought about her fun weekend with Mr. Tamerow. He'd spent hours teaching her to use the computer. Now she knew how to write a letter, locate a definition, scan the encyclopedia, find a rhyming word, and even how to create a pie chart.

To demonstrate the making of a pie chart, Mr. T. had asked Rilla to poll Harmony House guests with the question "Do you believe in Santa Claus?" The results:

Sparrow would be so impressed when her daughter turned in pie charts as part of home-schooler assignments. Hooray for easy extra credits.

The best part of Mr. Tamerow's computer lesson was learning how to use the modem to access the Internet. Fun! Except Mr. T. cautioned her about staying online too long since the service wasn't free.

The worst part of the weekend was saying goodbye to him last night. Rilla squinted at the clock. Seven. He was long gone by now—on his way to Helsinki.

"Helsinki," she grumbled, kicking off the sheet and scrambling out of bed. "Why can't Mr. T. get a different job and stop traveling so much?"

On her desk lay the pie chart they'd printed out

last night. It reminded her of how much fun she'd had online. *Mmm.* There was plenty of time to dress and get downstairs before class. *Let's see what's happening in cyberspace this morning.*

Rilla clicked on the computer. While it booted up, she snatched a shirt from her closet. The pocket was ripped. Oh well, she'd throw it into Aunt Poppy's mending basket later. While the modem dialed, she searched for her back-to-school jeans, but found the old ones with the tea stain instead.

Rilla brushed at the stain as she settled in at her desk.

WELCOME, EARTHGIRL7! the screen shouted.

earthgirl7 was her screen name. Mr. Tamerow had suggested Rilly, but she wanted to hide her true identity in case she said something dumb online. She wasn't sure what the 7 stood for. The service had assigned it to her. Maybe it meant six other earthgirls lived in cyberspace.

The tiny mailbox was blinking. She had e-mail!

Rilla wiggled the mouse around and clicked on the mailbox. The message was from **ABETAM**— Mr. Tamerow. He must have used his laptop computer and cellular phone to send her an early-morning message.

Surprise, Rilly!
Hugs to my favorite earthgirl.

Study hard this fall. I will return to Harmony House as soon as I Finnish in Helsinki. Get it? Ha ha ha.   ---->Mr. T.

Rilla laughed even though it was a horrible pun. Clicking on "Reply," she typed:

Got your message! Love my computer! Thanks a gazillion! Miss you already! Hope you Finnish soon! Ha ha, yourself!

After changing half the obnoxious exclamation points to periods, she signed "Rilla," then changed it to "earthgirl," adding an e-mail happy face: :)

Closing the mailbox, she scanned the Internet log for hobby topics.

Wow!

The list was a cyber mile long—baking bread, snowboarding, raising pigs, cycling, stamp collecting, Elvis-impersonating, TeenTown.

Mmm. TeenTown sounded like a fun place to explore.

Rilla glanced at the clock: seven forty-five. Time to hustle down to breakfast. But this was soooooo interesting.

She clicked on TeenTown. Instantly, the screen opened to a menu with a list of topics: books, sports, pets, and movies.

Rilla raced the clock, reading furiously, zipping e-mail responses to kids who shared her interests:

From: **earthgirl7**
To: **Katnip**
   I have four cats, too!

From: **earthgirl7**
To: **MuSiCaL**
   I play the ukulele. What do you play?

Clank, clank, clank.

That was Sparrow, banging a spoon on the pipes running from the kitchen to the attic. It meant "Get down here. You're late for breakfast."

Rilla exited to the main menu and started to sign off, but a list of "how to find" folders caught her eye: how to find rare coins, how to find fruits in season, how to find missing people. . . .

Whoa. *Missing people?*

Rilla's hand froze on the mouse. Missing people like her father?

He'd left before she was born, but had probably *tried* to find her, according to Sparrow. Surely his attempts were foiled by her mom's decision to change their last name (from Pinowski to Earth).

And by their various moves around the country before the Earth trio landed at Harmony House.

You vowed to find your father, her inner voice reminded her, *and you haven't done much about it.*

"I know." Rilla recalled making the vow after a recent mother-daughter talk with Sparrow. If her father *had* tried to find her and failed, maybe all he needed was a little help from this end. From her.

She touched the word "missing" on the screen. "I never knew where to start looking."

Why not here?

Rilla's hand trembled as she clicked on the folder. **Welcome to LAF Inc.,** the screen read. **Lost and Found Incorporated.**

Rilla thought it sounded like a place to locate lost mittens—not missing people.

After skimming a zippy story about how many people had located long-lost friends and relatives with the help of LAF Inc., she made up her mind to try it.

CLANK! CLANK! CLANK!

Hurry!

Quickly, Rilla filled in the blanks on a form titled **"Searcher"**:

Name of person
you wish to locate: **David Charles Pinowski**
Relationship: **Father**

Your name:	**Rilla Harmony Earth**
Name person knew you by:	**Rilla Pinowski**
Internet address:	**earthgirl7**

With a determined click, Rilla hit "Send," and off into cyberspace zoomed her precious information.

Then she crossed her fingers—even though it was awfully hard to type that way.

Morning Rush Hour

Rilla hurried down the back steps (the servants' stairway in the old days). Sparrow was writing today's lesson plan with one hand while feeding fresh oranges into a juicer with the other.

"Did you get the mail?" her mother asked.

Oops. Playing on the computer had been so engrossing, she'd forgotten to go down the street to the community boxes to fetch the other kind of mail. The kind with stamps that takes days to arrive instead of seconds.

"I'll get it during first break," Rilla promised.

Sparrow zapped another orange. "I know classes are just beginning, and it takes a while to get back into the swing of things, but the sooner, the better."

Rilla snatched a cinnamon pecan muffin from a

wicker basket. "It's only two minutes past eight. I'm not late."

"Hey, those muffins are for the guests. Yours are keeping warm in the oven." Sparrow tsked. "Now there's a hole in the basket. Replace the one you took."

Rilla obeyed, grabbing seconds for herself.

"*School* starts at eight, Rill—not breakfast." Sparrow poured the juice into a fancy pitcher just as Aunt Poppy flew through the kitchen, deposited a tray of dirty dishes, scooped up the muffin basket and pitcher, then headed back to attend to the guest table in the dining room.

Sparrow wiped her hands on a burlap apron that read *Feed the World.* "Sorry. Don't mean to be grouchy this morning. I'm running late, too, especially with my lesson plans."

"Not a problem. I'm your only student. I don't care if you're late."

"Need I remind you?" Sparrow paused to serve Rilla a plate of fruit pancakes made with soy flour. "We're starting the year off with group lessons."

Rilla choked on her first bite. *Group lessons? All the home-schoolers will be here? Including Joshua Banks?* She glanced at her ripped shirt and tea-stained jeans. *Rats.*

"Remember?" Sparrow added. "Last spring we

voted to meet more often as a group, *and* we voted to meet here since your classroom is larger than anyone else's."

If I did *remember,* Rilla grumbled to herself, *I would've spent less time online and more time on my appearance.*

Voices from the classroom told her Aunt Poppy had already let the home-schoolers inside. *Rats again.* Rilla made a mental note: *Look good on Mondays.*

"Finish your pancakes and get going."

Rilla speared the last blackberry, then dumped her plate into the sink.

Mornings were crazy at Harmony House. Aunt Poppy served breakfast to the B & B guests from seven to nine while Sparrow stayed in the kitchen, preparing food and getting a jump on the evening hors d'oeuvres, set out for guests from four to six o'clock.

At the same time, the super Earth Mother started Rilla's lessons. On group days, it was even crazier, although Mrs. Welter (mother of home-schooler Tina) took over for Sparrow as soon as she arrived.

Rilla stepped into the tiny bathroom behind the basement stairs to pull up the sides of her hair with a rubber band she found hooked over the doorknob. At least it made her look as though she'd spent more than two seconds getting ready for school this morning.

Tap-tap-tap.

"Someone's at the back door," she hollered to her mother.

"So open it."

Rilla peeked through the curtain. It was home-schooler Andrew Hogan. What was he doing slipping in the back? Trying to get in before someone noticed he was tardy?

"Hi," Rilla said, opening the screen door.

Andrew's gaze traveled from the tip of her head all the way to her sandals and back again. "Well, hel-l-l-l-oooo there." He wiggled his eyebrows up and down and grinned as if he knew a secret he wasn't going to tell.

It was such a dopey thing to say and do, yet it made Rilla nervous. *So* nervous that all the words she'd normally say evaporated from her brain.

Why?

Because he's flirting with you.

Rilla studied his face. *Andrew Hogan is flirting with me?*

"Sorry I'm late," he whispered in his soft Australian accent as he slipped past her. "Has class started?"

"Hello, Mr. Hogan," Sparrow called, giving him

a look that meant she knew why he was sneaking in the back. "You two get going. Tell Mrs. Welter I'll be there as soon as I put away the perishables."

Andrew motioned for Rilla to walk ahead of him as he gave her a smarmy grin.

What had gotten into him over the summer?

Straightening her torn pocket, Rilla put a hand over the tea stain on her jeans and hurried into the classroom.

Later she'd ponder this new, flirty Andrew Hogan.

Back to School

"Hi, Earth," greeted Joshua Banks (her one true love) the instant she stepped into the classroom.

It pleased her.

What *didn't* please her was the fact that Tina Welter had already grabbed the seat next to Joshua, sitting so close her shoulder touched his.

Rilla sat across the table, acting as if she didn't care.

Marcia Ruiz and Wally Pennington were playing a game on the computer. Andrew hurried to join them.

It seemed strange not to have Kelly Tonario here, but her parents had sent her to a private school this fall. Rilla missed Kelly's bubbly smile.

Settling in, she tried to stop thinking about Andrew and his weird behavior. Instead, she studied

Joshua Banks, who was acting equally weird. His gaze kept shifting between her and the wall calendar. Meanwhile, he pretended to be engrossed in Tina's blathering.

Rilla was confused. *Did he see Andrew flirting with me?*

Impossible.

Now Joshua was subtly pointing a finger at her, then the calendar.

Huh? Following his gaze, Rilla squinted at the date. Today was the last day of August. So what?

Ohhhhhh. Her brain, always groggy in the morning, realized what Joshua was trying to tell her. Tomorrow was the first day of September. The first day of a new month meant a new monster would arrive in the mail.

The September selection of the Monster of the Month Club.

Joshua Banks was the only person in the world who knew her monster secret. He knew because he'd accidentally found out about Burly, the May selection, so Rilla had to clue him in on the others.

On the first of June, Joshua had met her bright and early at the Earth mailbox, but Summer, the birdlike monster, had shown up stuffed.

Joshua'd been there on the first days of July and August, too, waiting to welcome Sparkler and Butterscotch—who'd also arrived stuffed, the way monsters were supposed to be.

Rilla glanced at her one true love, giving him a knowing nod to assure him she'd gotten his silent message. Now she knew what he was trying to tell her. He would meet her in the morning at the mailboxes.

Wally, Marcia, and Andrew finished their computer game and then joined the others at the table. Sparrow appeared, setting plates of warm fig granola on the table. Rilla ignored Tina's comments about "groan-ola" and gave Marcia a thankful smile for scooping up a cupful of the crunchy stuff without jeering, "At Wally's house we get chocolate doughnuts."

Rilla feared if someone spoke the words "chocolate doughnuts" out loud, the walls of Harmony House would come tumbling down.

"Okay, everybody." Mrs. Welter jabbed a witch-length fingernail at her students. "Here is our syllabus for this quarter, based on ideas and suggestions turned in last spring."

Perching on a stool made of olive wood, shipped (by Mr. T.) from Ankara, Turkey, Mrs. Welter began, "In math, we'll continue with geometry. History, we'll focus on life in medieval times. English literature, we'll be reading *Beowulf*. And in science, a unit on hydroponics."

Pausing, Mrs. Welter smiled at Joshua. "Hydroponics ties in with our group project, building the greenhouse in the Earths' backyard. I know you wanted to do a unit on astronomy, but we're saving that for next semester. A total eclipse will occur on Christmas Eve at the same time a comet passes earth. We plan to rent a high-powered telescope for the occasion."

Joshua looked disappointed by the delay. Rilla knew his interest in astronomy was solely due to the Legend of the Global Monsters: *When stars line up in angled shapes like lightning, real global monsters tread the earth once more.*

"Seeing all of these changes in the heavens will be a once-in-a-lifetime opportunity," Mrs. Welter added. "The last time anything like this happened was in the fifteenth century. You'll be surprised at how people explained what they were seeing. That's why we're studying medieval life this semester and medieval myths and legends next semester."

Rilla glanced at Joshua. The intrigued look on his face said, *Eclipse? Comet? Changes in the heavens? How does that relate to the monsters?*

Her curiosity matched his. Still, she worried that discovering too many scientific truths might ruin the magic. (She was way too superstitious.)

Sighing, Rilla caught Joshua's eye and

shrugged to let him know she shared his unspoken questions.

As troublesome as real monsters were in her life and her heart, the thought of *not* having them come to life in her attic made her too sad to ponder.

Monster in the Mail

Rilla had gotten lax about picking up the mail before school, waiting instead until first break when she was supposed to feed Taco and the cats.

But on this first day of September, curiosity pushed her out of bed before the alarm rang to meet the newest monster. And Joshua Banks.

The sight of him leaning against the Earth mailbox thrilled her more than Christmas morning. She squinted into the rising sun, trying to get a good look at her one true love: hair tumbling over his forehead, dimples in both cheeks, fingertips shoved into his jean pockets. Sigh.

"Hey, Earth," he called, flipping his bike out of the way so she could unlock the box.

"Hey, Banks," she answered.

Rilla's hand trembled as she turned the key. She

always expected a heavenly drumroll whenever she opened the box on the first morning of each month.

"Is it there?"

Joshua spoke in a hushed voice. Was he afraid the trees might overhear and whisper the monster secret to the rest of the neighborhood?

A ripple fluttered Rilla's heart when she spotted a package with foreign stamps.

Scooping up the rest of the mail, she dumped it into a cloth bag and thrust it at Joshua so she could draw out the monster box with both hands. Clutching it, she studied the mailing label. "Rangoon, Burma."

"Huh?" Joshua leaned over her shoulder to read it himself.

"Better not let Mrs. Welter know you've never heard of Burma," Rilla teased, although she, herself, had no clue where the country was located.

Joshua acted insulted. "Who said I never heard of it?"

Rilla could tell he was fudging by his twitchy eyebrows. "Come on," she said. "Let's go to the attic and meet the monster from Rangoon."

"Can't," Joshua said, glancing at his watch. "Open the package here."

Rilla gaped at him. "Here?"

"I don't have time to go to your house, then get home for class. My mom gets mad if I'm late."

Rilla understood home-schooling moms who hated tardiness.

Joshua gave her a pleading look that jiggled her heart. "Open it now so I don't have to wait till school's over to meet the monster. Pl-e-e-e-ase?"

Oh, those cute twisty brows; those double curvy dimples.

Rilla sighed. Joshua could've asked her to fly to Burma—sealed inside a monster box—and she would do it.

Reaching into his pocket, he whisked out a Swiss Army knife, smaller than Mr. Tamerow's.

Worried, Rilla glanced up and down the street. Passing cars paid them no mind. But what if somebody else came along to pick up mail? Somebody nosy like Tina Welter?

"Behind the bushes," Rilla ordered.

Before Joshua could argue, she threaded her way through the eight-foot hedge surrounding the house on the corner.

Inside, flower beds blanketed the yard, bordered by a smaller hedge. Perfect. Rilla dropped to her knees between the two hedges.

Joshua parked his bike, then slipped through the branches, eyeing windows of the house with guilt.

"Get down," Rilla told him.

He knelt, facing her. Setting aside the mailbag, he helped her cut the mailing tape.

Gingerly, Rilla released the top of the box. Rust-colored fur caught her eye. Fur that didn't appear to be moving.

Did you expect it to zoom out of the box and streak to the marigold bed?

Some of the monsters have, she reminded her inner voice.

Joshua was practically knocking her over, trying to get a look. "Take it out so I can see it," he urged.

"Wait." First she found the monthly selection card:

Monster of the Month Club
September Selection
Name: Owl   *Gender:* Male
Homeland: Rangoon, Burma
Likes: Poetry, numbers, literature
Never remove his glasses.

"This one must be smart," Rilla said. She lifted him from the box. He wasn't really an owl since he had pudgy arms and legs, but he *resembled* an owl: oversized head, rounded beak nose, small ears, and gigantic eyes—which looked even larger behind thick glasses.

"He must have lots of monster brains in that big head," Joshua joked.

"These look like real glasses." Rilla wiggled them to see if they'd come off. They would. But she didn't remove them. She knew from past experience to heed the warnings on selection cards.

Owl was dressed in a cap and gown, like a college professor on graduation day. His cap sported a rust tassel that matched his fur.

Mumbling, Joshua tossed a pebble into the bushes. "I *really* hoped this one would be . . ." His voice trailed off in disappointment.

Rilla knew what he meant. He'd loved playing with the May monster. June hadn't stayed alive very long, and July and August had remained stuffed. She knew he couldn't wait for another one to spring to life.

"Well, it's happened before," she reassured him. "It'll probably happen again."

"Or maybe not," he countered. "Maybe it'll *never* happen again."

Rilla shrugged. "It's all up to the stars."

Joshua poked the September monster in the tummy, as if wanting to confirm its stuffed state. "Yeah, well . . ." He tapped his watch. "I'd better get home." Bounding to his feet, he scooped up the mailbag.

Rilla dropped the selection card into the monster box. Straightening Owl's cardboard cap, she placed him inside and closed the lid, wishing there was something she could say to make Joshua feel better.

Handing over the mailbag, he pulled the bushes aside so Rilla could squeeze through.

"Ha, ha, ha, ha, ha."

Rilla stepped onto the sidewalk and turned to watch Joshua climb through the hedge. "What's so funny?"

He brushed leaves from his shirt. "I was going to ask you the same question."

"But I didn't laugh—you did."

Grabbing his bike, Joshua flipped up the kickstand and swung his leg over the seat. "No I didn't."

"Then who . . . ?" Rilla twirled. Had someone been spying on them?

"Ha, ha, ha, ha, ha."

THE BOX!

Rilla jerked it from under her arm and held it out in front of her. Laughter was coming from inside the monster box!

In Joshua's hurry to leap off his bike, he dumped it onto its side, scraping the metal against the sidewalk.

Rilla dropped to the ground, setting the box in the shade of the hedge. Her shaky hands could barely grasp the lid to open it.

Owl gazed up at them, huge eyes looking unreal beneath the thick lenses. Suddenly his nose began to twitch, sniffing the air like a dog.

"O-mi-gosh!" Rilla rasped.

Joshua's mouth was moving, but no words came out.

Owl gave them a magnified wink.

"Fooled ya," he teased. "Ha, ha, ha, ha, ha."

Owl-in-the-Box

Joshua and Rilla stared, open-mouthed, at the monster.

"He's alive!" Joshua sputtered.

"And he talked!" Rilla stammered. "None of them have ever talked before. I mean, in a language I could understand."

Owl sat up, turning his head side to side, like . . . well, like an owl.

"Oh, no you don't." Rilla grabbed his fuzzy arm to keep him from scrambling out of the box and dashing off into a world of humans who wouldn't cater to him the way she would.

He turned an intimidating gaze on her.

"I have to get you home before anybody sees you." She wondered if he understood her words.

"Hey, Jo-osh!" hollered a faraway voice.

Uh-oh. That snarly yell could belong to only one person.

Rilla leaned around Joshua to confirm her worst fear.

Tina Welter barreled toward them on her bike, coming to pick up mail for her mom.

"Distract her!" Rilla yelped. "I'll get the monster home."

Leaping to his feet, Joshua lifted his bike, blocking Tina's view of what was happening on the sidewalk behind him.

With quick apologies to the monster, Rilla slammed the lid on the Owl-in-the-Box. Dashing down Hollyhock Road, she made a beeline toward the privacy pines surrounding Harmony House's yard.

Slipping through the trees, Rilla raced across the grass.

"Hold still!" growled a muffled monster voice.

Rilla bent close to the box. "Sorry," she muttered, hoping no one saw her speaking to the mail. "Please don't say anything until we get to the attic. Then I'll let you out. I promise."

The monster grumbled; Rilla didn't catch what he said.

Bounding up the veranda steps, she pushed

through the double oak doors and tossed the mail-bag onto the sideboard. After racing up three flights of stairs (forty-seven steps), Rilla could barely catch her breath. Unlocking the door to the attic, she stumbled inside and dumped her armload onto the water bed.

Owl was out of the box in two seconds, grumping and arranging his professor gown and tassel. "Is this any way to treat a guest?" he humphed.

The sight of the mini-monster, trying to keep his balance on the ripply water bed while complaining in a squeaky Saturday-morning cartoon voice, was, to Rilla, hysterical.

She collapsed onto the bed, laughing.

Owl peered at her through glasses as thick as Coke bottles. "Is this the kind of manners one learns when one is home-schooled?"

Rilla's laugh lodged in her throat. "How did you know I'm home-schooled?"

Owl lifted one shoulder in what Rilla assumed was a monster shrug. "The home office doesn't send us out to just anybody."

"Wow." A zillion questions burst into Rilla's mind. But they'd have to wait. Sparrow had probably called LAF Inc. by now to report her daughter's disappearance.

"I have to get downstairs—um, to breakfast. Make yourself at home, and . . . and what do you eat?" She couldn't remember his card mentioning food.

Owl glanced around the attic. "Go," he said. "I can take care of myself."

Ha. Music to Rilla's ears. None of the other monsters had been able to take care of themselves. The September selection would be an easy one to keep.

Backing out the door, Rilla couldn't help but marvel at the monster miracle before her. On her way downstairs, she muttered, "Whoa," at least nine times, trying to adjust back to the real world— the one in which monsters didn't exist.

Sparrow was on the phone in the classroom. Slipping into the kitchen, Rilla grabbed a mug of papaya nectar and two of today's muffins (apple molasses), then returned to the classroom.

Opening a copy of *Beowulf,* she pretended to be incredibly absorbed by the ancient tale. A tale about a monster, no less.

Sparrow's furrowed brow told Rilla she wasn't off the hook. As soon as she hung up the phone, her mother's expression twisted into impatience. "Didn't we talk yesterday about being late?"

Oops.

"What time is it?" Sparrow demanded.

Rilla glanced at the earth clock above the door. The last three minutes of the hour were stick-figure people, showing that humanity had been on earth only three minutes out of earth's one-hour history. "Um, it's quarter after eight."

"Closer to twenty after," Sparrow corrected.

Rilla gestured toward the clock. "At least I showed up before the rest of humanity," she joked.

Her mother didn't laugh. "Why are you late?"

"I, um, ran into Joshua Banks at the mail-boxes." *The absolute truth,* she added to herself.

"Hmm." Sparrow peered over the top of her glasses with her pained "Please don't grow up and notice boys" look. Instead of answering, she plopped a fat notebook in front of her daughter. "This is your assignment folder for this semester, including worksheets. I'm grateful to Abe for finding us a home copier. It's so easy now to make worksheets."

Rilla set down her muffin to lift the notebook— a task which required both hands. "Obviously, it's a little *too* easy to make worksheets."

Sparrow ignored her. "Let's get started."

Sighing, Rilla flipped through the notebook. Page after page after page. *Ugh. Good thing Owl can take care of himself. Looks like I'll be way too busy this semester for monster-sitting. . . .*

Brain Food

Rilla didn't have time to feed Oreo and the kittens *and* check on the September monster during morning break. Since the hungry cats came first, it was noon before she had a chance to slip to the attic.

All morning, she'd felt guilty about not giving food to Owl. The other monsters demanded food—right now, hurry up, quick. What did Owl eat? She'd have to check his selection card again.

When Rilla got to the attic, Owl was perched on top of the dresser, hunched over the radio, yet no music was playing.

She stepped closer. Transistors and screws and knobs lay scattered across the dresser. "Oh, no! What are you doing?"

Owl gaped at her as though the answer was obvious. "Fixing it."

"But it wasn't broken." Rilla picked up a printed circuit board and groaned. "Put it back together."

"I'm trying."

"What do you mean, *trying*?"

"Taking it apart was easy. Putting it back together is hard."

Rilla sighed. So much for her radio.

Before double-checking Owl's birth announcement, she might as well download her e-mail. Maybe Mr. Tamerow had sent another message. Or maybe the lost-and-found folks had news for her.

Yikes.

Rilla turned on the computer and waited for it to boot up. That's when she noticed tiny pieces of paper scattered beneath the desk. "What's this?"

"Lunch," Owl answered.

She glanced across the room. Bits of paper lay sprinkled along the windows by the bookshelf. "What's that?"

"Breakfast."

Rilla dropped to her knees to piece the scraps together. "Hey, this is my booklet about Pikes Peak. Mr. Tamerow sent it from Colorado." She glared at Owl. "You ate my booklet."

"Named after Zebulon Pike, who climbed half-way up the mountain in 1806," Owl stated. "Elevation, 14,110 feet."

Rilla stared at him. "You *ate* the booklet and now you *know* all about Pikes Peak?"

"A nine-mile cog railway shuttles tourists to the top," Owl answered.

"Amazing." Fetching the monster card, Rilla confirmed her suspicion. " 'Likes: poetry, numbers, literature.' Oh, I get it. Likes to *eat* them, not *read* them."

This was so incredible, it gave Rilla a crazy idea. Dashing downstairs, she hustled to the last suite on the blue floor—the one without a number.

Aunt Poppy, phone at her ear, opened the door. "Yeah?"

"Can I borrow a book?"

Her aunt nodded, laughing at something the person on the other end of the line had said.

Rilla headed for the bookcase, running her fingers along book spines. "How to repair . . . A to D," she read. "E to H."

"Hang on a minute, José." Aunt Poppy held the phone away from her ear. "What are you looking for?"

Rilla grinned. "Are you talking to José?"

José was a musician from Montana and a frequent guest at Harmony House. Rilla suspected her aunt had a major crush on him—which was funny since her aunt had already been married four times. Earth was her sixth surname. The other five were Knox Bailey Hailey Hobbs Street.

Aunt Poppy faked a grumpy face. "Like who I'm talking to is any of your business."

"Rilla, I need to borrow your book on radio repair."

Aunt Poppy pulled the Q-to-T volume off the shelf and tossed it to Rilla. "What?" she asked José. "Yes, it's my intolerable niece." Pausing, she handed the phone to Rilla. "José wants to say hello."

"Hi! This is the intolerable niece," Rilla quipped. "When are you coming to visit? Okay. Okay. Okay."

Aunt Poppy grabbed for the phone. "Hey, it's *my* turn to say okay, okay, okay."

"Bye, José!" Rilla hollered. "I'll e-mail you!"

Tucking the book beneath her arm, Rilla headed downstairs to the photocopier behind the registration desk, copied the pages on how to assemble a radio, then hurried to the attic.

Owl was working away, yet radio parts still lay scattered around the empty frame.

"Here." Rilla handed him the copied pages. "Have a snack."

Owl's eyes lit up. Dropping the volume knob, he began to gobble the pages.

Rilla sat at the computer and signed on to the Internet. The modem didn't connect. *Oh, right. Aunt Poppy is on the phone.*

While waiting, she cleaned up the half-eaten paper by the windows to see what Owl had eaten for breakfast. "Page 213 of my dictionary?"

"Getaway," Owl answered. "To flee after a crime. Geyser. A natural spring spouting hot water and steam. Gibbon. A long-armed ape."

"That's incredible," Rilla stammered. "Hurry up and finish your snack."

Returning to the computer, she tried again. This time the modem connected. The tiny electronic mailbox was blinking. "I've got mail!"

She clicked on her messages:

From: Katnip
To: earthgirl7
My cats' names are Minty,
Mason, Milford, and Mooney.
What are your cats' names?

Rilla clicked on "Reply" and typed: **Oreo, Dorito, Pepsi, and Milk Dud.**

The next message was from **MuSiCaL:**

Why did you ask if I play an instrument? Why do you think I care that you play the ukulele? I think you're weird.

So much for **MuSiCaL.** Rilla hit "Delete."

Suddenly music blasted from the radio, making her jump.

"You did it!" Rilla yelped, rushing to crank down the volume.

"The snack helped," Owl replied modestly.

Clank! Clank! Clank!

Oops. Time to get downstairs for afternoon lessons.

"I'll be back later," she told Owl, signing off the Internet. "If you get hungry, please wait till I can make a copy of your snack so you don't eat all my books."

He gave her a look that meant he didn't understand—or care.

Worried, she nabbed the latest issue of *'Teen* from a wicker basket and ripped out a page, glancing to see what it was: "September Horoscope." "Here's something you can snack on," she told him.

"I've already read it."

Rilla was downstairs before she realized that she hadn't received a reply from LAF Inc. How disappointing.

What if the online effort to find her father was nothing more than a random shot into cyberspace? What if she never heard back from LAF Inc.? Or worse, what if she never heard from her father?

Then again, what if she did?

10

Monster Games

The minute school was over for the day, Rilla dashed outside to check on Taco and the cats. Having a live monster in the attic meant less time to play with her pets—the ones who were *supposed* to be alive.

Aunt Poppy lounged on the patio, writing in a notebook. Taco lay half in, half out of her lap. All four cats were in attendance—one on Aunt Poppy's shoulder, the rest stalking a parade of ants along a crack in the cement.

Rilla felt pleased to see her aunt bonding with Taco. "What are you doing?" she asked.

Aunt Poppy slammed the notebook shut when she realized Rilla was peering over her shoulder. "Oh, uh, making a few notes."

Rilla thought she was acting guilty. "So, what's up?"

"Nothing. What makes you think something's up?"

Mmm. Rilla sat on the patio and gave Taco's neck a good rubbing. Her curiosity was piqued, yet Aunt Poppy was certainly entitled to harbor secrets just as much as she was.

Suddenly a bike came flying down the alley, skidded sideways, and barreled into the backyard.

Her one true love.

Joshua's jaw dropped when he spotted Taco in the presence of Aunt Poppy. Speaking of secrets . . .

Rilla knew Joshua's frantic arrival had nothing to do with Taco. He must have bolted the minute his mom dismissed him from class. Racing to Harmony House to play with the newest monster.

Taco galloped across the yard, meeting Joshua halfway, yipping and jumping to greet him. Joshua hopped off his bike, kneeling to fuss over the dog while shooting puzzled glances at Rilla.

Joining him, she quickly explained how her aunt had discovered Taco, and how the dog wasn't a secret anymore. She couldn't decide if Joshua looked relieved or disappointed. Now he wouldn't have to sneak into the barn to smuggle Taco to Willow Park for exercise.

Joshua roughed up the dog, rolling on the grass with him.

Rilla felt jealous. Taco didn't go crazy like that over her. Of course, she didn't play with him as much as Joshua did.

Aunt Poppy wandered over to talk about the soon-to-arrive, prefab greenhouse, and how great it would be to have fresh vegetables year-round, picked from their own backyard.

Joshua was polite, yet Rilla could tell he *really* wanted to head for the attic. Whipping a small notebook from his back pocket, he said, "Can we go over the geometry problems from Chapter Three?"

Rilla grinned. He was one step ahead of her. "My stuff's in the attic," she said for Aunt Poppy's benefit.

"Okay." Joshua's lips twitched as he tried not to smile.

Rilla led him inside and up the back steps, glad Sparrow was at the registration desk, checking in afternoon arrivals. Taco tried to come along with them, but Aunt Poppy held him back. Sparrow never allowed animals inside the B & B in case any guests were allergic.

Rilla hoped no one was sensitive to rust-colored monster fur.

Upstairs, she expected to find Owl napping, which is how most M.O.T.M. Clubbers spent their afternoons.

Instead, she found him at the computer.

Rilla froze. She remembered leaving the computer on—but had she signed off the Internet before dashing downstairs?

"Uh-oh."

Joshua slipped past, joining Owl at the desk.

"W-what's he doing?" Rilla crept forward, afraid to look.

Joshua peered at the screen. "Playing a game."

"A game." Rilla breathed a sigh of relief. Owl wasn't running up the Earths' online account after all. *Whew.*

"It's . . . it's . . ." Joshua paused, following Owl's quick movements as he zapped a one-eyed cyclops.

"Monster Munch," Owl answered.

Rilla chuckled. Leave it to a monster to find a monster game.

"Can I play?" Joshua asked.

Owl stopped the game and hit "Restart." Typing with paws looked awkward. Owl didn't appear very swift at it.

Maybe she should feed him her *How to Master*

Typing booklet for a bedtime snack, but she suspected he'd already found and devoured it.

Dragging over an extra chair, she joined the game.

Playing Monster Munch with a real monster—and her one true love—was much more entertaining than geometry.

☙1 ☙1
Surfin' the Net

After Joshua left, Rilla hurried downstairs to make copies of Mrs. Welter's review sheets and reading assignments from her textbooks.

These she fed to Owl for supper.

The monster's dessert included copied pages from Rilla's geometry book and *Beowulf*. While he ate, she signed on to the Internet and checked her mail. A letter from ABETAM!

> **Hi, Rilly! Arrived in the "Land of the Midnight Sun" in the midst of night— but it was still daylight. Fabulous view of the Baltic Sea from my hotel room. More later------>Mr. T.**

Wow. Day in the "midst of night." If the sky stayed light twenty-four hours, no stars would shine—or line up in angled shapes like lightning. Did that mean no monsters could spring to life in northernmost Finland this time of year?

Maybe in winter, when twenty-four hours of darkness ruled and stars shone night and day, Finland spawned monsters galore. Who knows?

Rilla clicked the mouse on the next message:

From: Katnip
To: earthgirl7
              Your cats have strange names!
              I have one brother and two
              sisters, and I go to Kingston
              Middle School. Where do you
              go?

Rilla hit "Reply":

I am home-schooled. I don't have any
brothers or sisters.

She started to type, **I have a pet monster,** but thought better of it.

Rilla was itching to write a letter to José. He'd given her his e-mail address when they talked on Aunt Poppy's phone.

From: earthgirl7
To: GuitarGuy
              José, it's me—Rilla! How do you

**like my screen name? Where is
your next gig?**

After hitting "Send," the computer voice said,
"You've got mail."

Someone was e-mailing her this very second.
How exciting!

The letter was from a name she didn't recognize:
TwoBad:

**You are on the LAF Inc. list of
daughters looking for their fathers. I
am a father looking for my daughter.
Don't know her married name. Was
hoping it was Earth. She'd be 35 years
old now. Are you my Rilla?**

Wow. Another lost father and daughter—and
the girl's name was Rilla. Reading the letter made
her feel sad for her namesake.

She clicked on "Reply" and typed: **No, I am
not your Rilla. I am only 13.** Then she added,
I'm not married. "Too bad, TwoBad," Rilla whispered, sending the message along with her sympathy.

So. There was a whole *list* of fathers and daughters trying to connect. It surprised Rilla to think of
others in cyberspace, also searching.

One more letter in her electronic mailbox.

From: MonsterKid
To: earthgirl7
No, I am not a real monster.
Why did you ask such a dumb
question? MonsterKid is just
my screen name.

Rilla's heart skittered. This was not the answer to any question *she* had asked. This was the answer to "Are you a real monster?" A question *asked* by a real monster.

"Owl!"

The September selection sprawled on the water bed, scribbling on the worksheets she'd given him.

"You went online and used my screen name to send e-mail!"

Owl adjusted his glasses and gazed at her. "Mars will enter your sign on the tenth. Money will be tight, but creativity will get you by. Someone new will enter your life. He will be a puzzle."

Rilla scrunched her face at him. "What are you talking about?"

Then she remembered. The snack. He'd eaten the horoscope page from *'Teen*. "Oh, geez," Rilla muttered.

Owl scrambled off the bed and fetched the online manual from a desk drawer. Jagged bite-shaped pieces were missing.

Oh, great. The horoscope page wasn't enough. The monster had also nibbled enough knowledge to surf the Net.

"No, no, no." Rilla snatched the manual away, even though a sinking feeling told her it was too late. "Playing games on the computer is fine," she told him. "Going online is not. Promise you won't do it again."

Owl gave her a pitiful look.

Had her scolding worked? He *seemed* sorry. "Try to forget what you ate—um, I mean, well, you know what I mean."

Owl handed her the completed worksheets. One was her geometry homework with all the answers neatly penciled in. The other was an essay she was supposed to write on *"Beowulf:* Why Twentieth-Century Students Still Study a Poem from the Eighth Century."

Rilla caught her breath as she read the essay, written in perfect English in an unusual style of handwriting. Square N's and W's. Loopy P's and R's. Is this the way English penmanship was taught in Burma?

The absurdity of it all threatened to overrule Rilla's awe. Gently, she grasped the monster's paw. "I'd hoped you'd *help* me with my homework, but you *did* it for me. All of it. How can I ever repay you?"

Owl tapped his other paw on the keyboard and wiggled his nose.

"Ohhhhh. You want to trade time online for homework?"

Sparrow's words popped into Rilla's mind: *It's against my better judgment.* That's what she'd said about keeping Taco.

But this was too good to pass up. *I'll be free from homework in exchange for a little online monster surfing. Mmm.*

"It's a deal," Rilla said, shaking his paw to make it official. "On the condition that you only go online when I'm sitting here beside you."

Rilla grinned at him. She wasn't crazy. She was way too smart to let a monster loose in cyberspace. . . .

12

The Greenhouse Effect

Rilla burst out the back door of Harmony House.

Late again.

The home-schoolers were gathered on the newly poured concrete slab in the Earths' backyard, waiting to assemble the greenhouse that arrived yesterday from the HomeGrown Company in British Columbia.

Rilla blamed her tardiness on e-mail and the need to find something good for Owl's breakfast. (A page from her science text explaining hydroponics—whatever *that* was.) These were excuses she could not offer any teacher, so she was pleased to find Mrs. Welter and Aunt Poppy busily ripping open HomeGrown cartons.

Rilla shivered. Glancing at the overcast sky, she wished she'd put on a sweater. The arrival of September on the calendar always seemed to drop the mercury fifteen degrees.

Aunt Poppy, wearing her *Think Green* sweat-shirt, and Mrs. Welter in her faux fur jacket, finished stacking clear plastic panels on the grass, then began to organize home-schoolers into work crews.

Sparrow flew out the door, stopping Rilla before she could join the others. "See this?" She pointed at the doormat—or what *used* to be the mat. Now it was a pitiful pile of shredded rubber.

"What happened?"

"In a word," Sparrow answered, "Taco."

Rilla picked up a piece of flat rubber with the letter V on it. "Taco chewed up the mat Mr. Tamerow sent from Italy?" (Upon entering, it read *Ave!* and leaving, *Vale!*, Latin for "Hail!" and "Farewell!")

"Plus the hose," Sparrow added, "and a garden glove I forgot to take inside." She waved the un-chewed glove at her daughter. "After school, please go to Mr. Baca's and buy rubber dog toys so Taco will have his own toys to chew on."

Rilla nodded, wondering if she'd have to dip into her allowance to pay for the damage.

"If you pay for the toys, I'll replace the items Taco ruined."

Bingo.

Rilla jogged across the lawn to join the home-schoolers, feeling thankful a dog had done the damage and not a monster.

"Well, hel-l-l-l-oooo," Andrew said, greeting her.

The entire group froze on cue to see who Andrew was addressing. When they saw it was only Rilla, they returned to their activities.

Except for Joshua Banks. His gaze, under a furrowed brow, began to shift suspiciously between Andrew and Rilla.

"Geez," Rilla muttered. *This could get uncomfortable.*

Mrs. Welter divided the group into two teams—planners and assemblers. Rilla was an assembler, along with Marcia and Andrew, who kept grinning at her, goofy-like. Tina ended up on the opposite team—with Joshua, of course.

Mrs. Welter barked commands. The assemblers assembled. The planners sat on the lawn and chatted.

"Not fair," Rilla griped.

Finally Sparrow joined the planners to discuss how to arrange the inside of the greenhouse once the walls were up and the roof was on.

Tomatoes, cucumbers, greens, sprouts, carrots, and onions would grow year-round, providing the B & B guests with fresh, organically grown salads and veggies. Flowers would be planted, too, for aesthetics (and oxygen). One corner would be set aside for the home-schooler hydroponics experiment.

The assemblers spent the next hour snapping poles into place, tightening screws, climbing up and down ladders, and lifting squares of see-through plastic into position. Finally, the planners joined in to expedite the task—not as simple as the directions made it sound.

Tina kept doing three things that bugged Rilla:

1. Wiggling in between her and Joshua whenever they happened to be working side by side.

2. Stopping to play with Milk Dud, who seemed to think the entire project was being done to entertain him.

3. Making snide remarks about the Earth family (like "*Normal* people buy vegetables at a grocery store").

The only amusing part of the day was when Tina backed into an anchor pole and kerplopped onto her bottom in the mud.

"Break time," Sparrow called. "Round up your worksheets on hydroponics and we'll meet on the patio to discuss."

Uh-oh. Rilla had left her worksheet with Owl. "May I run up to my room and get a jacket?" she asked. "I'm getting cold."

Sparrow glanced at the gray sky, grumbling

about the weather not being conducive to a solar greenhouse. "Be quick," she answered.

Dashing upstairs, Rilla whipped into the attic, slamming the door. "Did you finish my worksheet?" she hollered at Owl as she dove into her closet to fetch a jean jacket. (She'd embroidered the earth on the back with a kit Aunt Poppy had given her last Christmas.)

Fumbling with the coat hanger, Rilla untangled it and tossed it onto the rug to deal with later. Then she slid onto the bed, making waves roll. She really *was* trying to hurry for Sparrow's sake.

Owl held out the worksheet as Rilla struggled into her jacket. She snatched it from his paw. All the answers were in perfect order. "This is so great!" she chirped.

Rilla lunged to hug him. That's when she noticed what Owl was doing.

Playing cards.

With a monster.

A *live* monster.

Dressed in a peasant frock, sandals, and love beads.

Rilla froze mid-hug. "B-Butterscotch?! You're alive!"

The expression on the she-monster's face was one of terror. Cards flipped from both paws and rained across the quilt. Scrambling over the other stuffed animals on Rilla's pillow, Butterscotch dove off the side.

"Oh, I scared you!" Rilla scuttled around the bed just in time to see the August monster disappear beneath the quilt.

"Way to go," Owl mumbled. "Just when I was about to win."

Excited, Rilla jumped up and down three times. "Wow, another live monster! Wait till Joshua hears—Oh, rats. I'd better get downstairs or Sparrow will ground me for the rest of the month."

Clutching the worksheet, she backed toward the door. "Owl, talk to Butterscotch. Tell her not to be afraid of me. Say I'm her, um, caretaker, guardian, mother—whatever. Please?"

Owl gave her a crooked grin. A monster-plotting-his-own-agenda type of grin. She'd seen it before on other monster faces and knew it wasn't a good kind of grin.

"Please?" Rilla pleaded before closing the door. The talking monster chose not to answer.

13

Rule
Number
One

As the home-schoolers carried extra chairs to the patio, an excited Rilla tried to corner Joshua and give him up-to-the-minute monster news.

Unfortunately, Tina stayed glued to Joshua, no matter how hard Rilla tried to draw him away. Tina's crabby frown remained fixed on Rilla, as if she suspected the Earth girl was up to something.

The Earth girl *was* up to something, but Tina would never find out in a million trillion years.

Rilla dashed inside for one more chair. Stopping in the kitchen, she ripped the bottom off Sparrow's grocery list and printed one word in capital letters: AUGUST!!!

As the group settled in on the patio, Rilla slipped the note to Joshua.

In a heartbeat, Tina was hanging over his shoulder. "What's *that* supposed to mean?"

Rilla watched slow realization light Joshua's face as the note's meaning sunk in. Grinning, he shoved the paper into his pocket.

It drove Tina crazy. She whisper-hissed into Joshua's ear, but all he'd do was shrug and shake his head.

Rilla laughed out loud, drawing curious glances, but she didn't care. She and her one true love could communicate almost without words. Sigh.

Mrs. Welter began to lecture. Rilla focused on the lesson, but her thoughts remained in the attic.

Colorful Butterscotch had sprung to life! The August monster, whose motionless arrival had been a mere month ago. Rilla remembered her delight with the monster from Nepal who liked honey, granola, and tofu—three foods easy to find at Harmony House. Not a penny of her allowance would go toward *this* monster's food.

But she's afraid of you.

Rilla pictured the August birth announcement: Shy. Needs lots of peace and quiet.

No wonder she's afraid of me. I slammed into the attic, hollered at Owl, tossed a coat hanger across the room, plopped onto the bed, and grabbed her playmate.

Rilla sighed. *I'll have to win her trust. Maybe with food?*

"Earth to Earth," Sparrow said, jabbing her daughter on the shoulder. "Mrs. Welter is talking to you."

Rilla tidied her mind of monsters and focused on the present.

Tina snickered loud and clear, nudging Wally to join her.

Wally was too busy reviewing his worksheet to snicker with Tina, which made Rilla grateful.

"I asked," Mrs. Welter repeated in her tactful tone, "if you would please give us a basic definition of hydroponics?"

"Sure." Rilla gulped. The definition was right here in her hand. The *problem* was that she hadn't written it, meaning she needed to *read* it before she could spout it with authority.

Rilla buried her nose in the worksheet and began, "Hydroponics is the science of—"

"Stop." Mrs. Welter whisked the worksheet from her grasp.

Uh-oh. Rilla's heart began to pound.

The teacher waved the worksheet in the air like a warning flag. "We've tried to impress upon each of you that these are meant to be a tool to help you research. When we gather to discuss the topic, you should be prepared to talk without having to read from your notes."

All the home-schoolers turned toward Rilla, acknowledging the fact that she was being featured as a bad example.

Rats. She hated getting scolded in front of everybody.

"Take two, Rilla," Mrs. Welter quipped. "Let's begin with a definition. That shouldn't be too hard, should it?"

Not if I'd done my own homework.

Rilla had no idea what hydroponics meant because Mrs. Welter hadn't given her time to finish reading the sentence. The sentence Owl had written.

"Um." Now she felt warm enough to remove her earth jacket—which she did to stall for time. Rubbing the side of her nose (which didn't help at all), she squinted at Mrs. Welter. "I can't remember."

Sparrow began to study the charcoal sky again, although Rilla knew her thoughts weren't on the weather. They were on how much her daughter was humiliating her right now.

"When you do research," Mrs. Welter began in her incredibly patient voice, "you do three things. One, *read* the information. Two, *write* it on the worksheet. Three, *review* it before we meet. That's three shots at sinking the facts into your brain."

Silence on the patio grew so loud, it pained Rilla's ears. *Would somebody please change the subject?*

"Marcia," Mrs. Welter said. "Give me the ol' one, two, three."

Marcia offered Rilla a sympathetic smile. "Read, write, and review."

"Correct," said Mrs. Welter, gesturing with all ten manicured nails as if her inch of polish hadn't dried yet. "Now. About hydroponics."

Wally wiggled his hand in the air. "I know, I know."

You always know, Rilla scoffed. *But you don't have monsters in your attic to distract you. None of you do.*

Still, a tiny seed of guilt began to grow inside of her. *Face the music, Earth. You didn't do your homework.*

Wasn't my fault, she argued feebly to herself. *I didn't ask Owl to do it.*

Mrs. Welter studied Rilla's worksheet. "You know, you answered these questions beautifully." After a beat, she added, "I think," then passed the worksheet to Sparrow. The two whispered together.

"This isn't your handwriting," Sparrow blurted.

Rilla wished Mrs. Welter's tactfulness would rub off on her mother.

"I was, um, experimenting." *True,* she added to

herself. *Experimenting with a monster doing my homework.*

Sparrow leaned over Joshua's shoulder and scrutinized his worksheet. Comparing handwriting? Did Sparrow think Joshua had done her homework? *Geez.*

"Go, Wally," Sparrow said. "Tell Rilla and the rest of us about the experiment we'll be conducting in our greenhouse." Giving her daughter a baffled frown, she dropped the worksheet into Rilla's lap as if eager to get rid of it.

Rilla bent over the worksheet, letting her hair fall forward to hide her face. She followed along while Wally recited the exact words Owl had written.

"Hydroponics is the science of growing plants in nutrient-enriched water instead of soil."

"Very good." Sparrow patted Wally's shoulder as she passed behind his chair but her gaze remained on Rilla. "Other substances, like gravel, can be used, but we'll focus on the use of water."

Rilla pivoted her chair away from the group to ignore Sparrow's frowns and Tina's exasperated sniffing.

Rule number one, she told herself. *After Owl does your homework, READ it before going to class. . . .*

14

Guess Who's Coming to Dinner?

Rilla thought the home-schoolers would never leave. Especially Andrew. He hung around forever, as if he wanted to be alone with her.

Ironically, Joshua was hanging around for the same reason. Well, not *exactly*. He wanted to be alone with Rilla so he could race to the attic and meet the newest monster who'd come to life.

Finally, Andrew gave up and went home. Seconds later, Rilla and Joshua hit the attic stairwell. "Don't move fast or make loud noises," she warned. "Butterscotch is skittish."

As the door swung open, a blondish blur streaked across the room and dove under the bed.

"See what I mean?" Rilla told him.

Joshua looked confused. "But I thought you said the *August* monster came to life."

"I did." Rilla followed his gaze—then sucked in a breath at the sight before her: a floppy-eared, red-white-and-blue monster, dressed in denim, playing Monster Munch with Owl.

"Sparkler?!"

Leaping to his furry feet, the startled July monster hung over the back of the chair, shooting Rilla a perplexed stare.

"Look!" Joshua cried. "He reacted to his name."

Even though Rilla thought Sparkler's patriotic fur clashed with rusty Owl, she loved his droopy ears.

Joshua edged closer. "Hello?" he asked as if he expected a civilized answer.

Sparkler rubbed his tummy.

"He's hungry," Rilla and Joshua chimed in unison.

Rilla couldn't remember what the July monster ate. While she fetched his selection card, Joshua dropped to the floor and lifted a corner of the quilt. "Hi, Butter," he cooed. "Want some dinner?"

"Hot dogs, chips, and apple pie," Rilla muttered, wondering how she was supposed to round up food that was so anti–Harmony House.

Sparkler jumped up and down on the chair. "Scree-UK! Scree-UK!"

Uh-oh. Here come the loud noises his card warned about.

Owl, who hadn't missed a beat playing the game, finally stopped to grace Rilla with an annoyed glower. "He wants food."

"No kidding." Rilla wished all the monsters' diets consisted of items in the attic, like Owl's. On second thought—what if one devoured sheets and blankets? Clothes? Computers? *Yikes. Never mind.*

Rilla nudged Joshua's leg. "Can we talk?"

His head came out from under the quilt. Acting embarrassed, he rose to his knees, smoothing ruffled hair.

"I think I'm going to need help feeding these two," Rilla told him.

"No problem. What does Butterscotch eat?"

"I can take care of her food—honey, granola, and tofu."

At the mention of August monster food, a tiny wail echoed from beneath the bed. It sounded like a lost kitten crying for its mama.

Rilla's heart turned over. "Soon, Butter," she called, copying the nickname Joshua had given her.

"Me-yup," the monster answered.

At least she's talking to me. . . .

Rilla showed Sparkler's card to Joshua. "If I give you money, will you go to Mr. Baca's and—oh, wait. They sell frozen pies. How can I . . . ?"

Joshua snapped his fingers. "I'll swing by Mc-Donald's and buy one of their apple pies."

"Great." Rilla lifted her unhappy-panda bank off the dresser. The pouting bear wore a shirt that read *It's Sad to Be Endangered*. She shook coins and bills into Joshua's hand, unsure how much to give him.

"That's enough." He shoved the money into his pocket. "I feel like the monsters are *my* responsibility, too, so I'll make up the difference."

"Are you sure?"

He shrugged. "We both know the legend is true, so we're sorta in this together. I mean, it's our secret, right?"

He gave her such a kind look, Rilla felt like crying. It was one of the nicest things anyone had ever said to her.

As soon as Joshua left, Rilla scooted Owl out of the way so she could play with Sparkler. But the July monster sprang from the chair, grabbed his skateboard, and zoomed back and forth across the hardwood floor.

Click-clack, click-clack, click-clack.

Rilla knew there was no way she could make him *not* do what he was programmed to do. "Please tell me no one downstairs can hear the click-clacking," she mumbled to the computer screen.

Owl climbed onto the bed and settled down to

nibble on last week's *TV Guide,* which Rilla had carried to the attic along with the Sunday paper.

"Are you starting dinner without waiting till your friends are served?" she teased. "Bad monster manners, Owl."

He ignored her.

Rilla knew she should hustle downstairs for Butterscotch's food, but now was her chance to do what she'd been dying to do all day—find out if e-mail had arrived from José, Mr. Tamerow, or—gulp—her father.

Hurry, hurry, hurry, she urged as the modem dialed and connected her computer to the globe, as Mr. Tamerow would say.

How she loved blinking mailboxes!

From: **GuitarGuy**
To: **earthgirl7**
I will arrive at Harmony House tomorrow.
A big surprise awaits you!

"Oh, goody, José is coming! I love surprises."

From: **MonsterMom**
To: **earthgirl7**
No, I am not a real monster. I am the mother of quadruplets,

**and sometimes I *feel* like a
monster. Hope you were joking.
You're not *really* a monster,
are you?**

"Ow-wul . . ." Rilla groaned. "You're only allowed to go online when I'm here, remember?"

He answered by biting the head off George Clooney (on the cover of *TV Guide*).

"No message from Mr. Tamerow," Rilla grumbled. "And no message from the lost-and-found folks." She zipped a quick message to Helsinki—**Wanted to say hi!**—and one to LAF Inc.—**Any news about my father?**

Click-clack, click-clack, click-clack.

The July monster was annoying her, but she sympathized with him. After all, he hadn't been fed since leaving . . . Hong Kong? Whoa. Better keep the details straight—three countries, three menus, three "warnings."

Her screen name should be MonsterMom—ha!

Rilla's sense of duty made her exit from cyberspace and hustle down to the pantry to round up Butterscotch's dinner before Joshua returned.

Never before had two monsters sprung to life in one day. The thrill should have kept her wired for weeks. But the thrill was overshadowed by the lack of mail from LAF Inc.

What she would give to read those words again: "Are you my Rilla?"

Only next time she wanted the question to come from the one person to whom she could answer emphatically: "YES!"

An answer she'd been waiting to give for thirteen years.

15

Bedtime in the Attic

"Come on," Rilla cooed.

Flat on her stomach, head beneath the quilt, she held out a tiny saucer of fig granola and crumbled tofu, drizzled with honey.

Butterscotch edged close, reaching a paw toward the plate.

Rilla drew it away, letting the quilt fall between them.

"I'm not trying to be cruel," she said in her softest voice. "I just want you to trust me."

It reminded Rilla of last fall when Oreo took up residence under the veranda steps. The only way she could earn Oreo's trust was to coax her out with food. Then Rilla carried the mama cat to the barn to show her a better place to live—warm, dry, and away from October's bone-chilling weather. All in all, a good place to raise her future family.

Butterscotch peeked from beneath the quilt.

"Yes," Rilla urged. "Come out. I won't hurt you."

Owl, acting aggravated, flopped over the side of the bed and jabbered at Butterscotch in an unknown tongue.

She prattled an answer, then boldly crawled out from under the bed and sat cross-legged, waiting for dinner to be served.

Rilla placed the saucer on the rug in front of her. "Look, Owl, Butter understood you."

Owl rolled back onto the bed, like it was no big deal.

"Is there a universal monster language?"

"Monster lingo," Owl answered.

"Yeah, really?" Rilla was fascinated. "Go on."

"Today. On Oprah."

Rilla groaned. *Thank you,* TV Guide.

The sound of footsteps coming up the attic stairs made her heart beat faster. Her one true love was back—with monster food.

Sparkler's nose knew what was in the bag before Joshua opened it. While they watched, he devoured three cold hot dogs, a small bag of chips, and the apple pie, still warm.

Joshua pulled hot dog buns from the sack, giving Rilla a sheepish grin. "Didn't know if he needed these."

"Guess you'd better take them home," she told him. "My mom has never served hot dogs in the history of Harmony House."

"What about the leftover meat?" Joshua asked. "It'll spoil."

"No it won't. I have a cooler. I'll bring ice up from downstairs." Rilla chuckled as she remembered *why* she once needed a cooler—to keep the January monster's frozen foods icy cold.

Joshua handed her a grocery sack bearing the logo from Mr. Baca's One-Stop Shoppette. The bag contained enough food for several days. "It's getting late," he said. "I'd better go home."

"Thanks for helping."

Joshua absently jiggled the doorknob instead of turning it. "I ran into Andrew at the store."

Rilla heated up. "You did?"

"He asked me if you, uh, well . . ." Joshua paused to straighten a throw rug with his shoe. "If you, um, liked him."

Mixed emotions swirled through Rilla's heart. Part of her was flattered by the attention, and part of her didn't want Joshua to be scared away.

He avoided her eyes. "So, uh, *do* you?"

She giggled, making Joshua giggle, too. Nervously.

"As a friend."

Joshua looked relieved. He opened the door.

"Wait." Rilla grabbed his sleeve. "So what did you tell him? When he, um, asked if I liked him?"

Joshua acted as if he'd rather answer any other question in the universe—except that one. "I told him . . . no way." He grinned, making his double dimples appear. Half moons carved in both cheeks.

They laughed again. Rilla thought he held her gaze a few beats longer than comfortable. But she didn't mind. Not a bit.

Andrew was okay, but Joshua, *he* was her one true love.

Getting ready for bed was a major ordeal. Last night, Owl had slept in the rocking chair buried beneath stuffed animals, so that's where he settled in tonight.

What was she supposed to do with the other two (uninvited) B & B guests? Rent out suites for them on the blue floor? Ha!

Rilla fixed a bed for Butterscotch in the bottom drawer of the dresser. Unfortunately, the monster retreated to "underland" instead.

Oh, well. Rilla wadded up bath towels and

shoved them under the bed. Later when she checked, Butterscotch had mooshed the towels together to create a comfy bed. "Night, Butter," Rilla whispered.

"Mi-thrup," answered the monster.

Rilla chuckled. "She's taking a liking to me!"

Groans echoed from beneath the stuffed-animal pile.

"Hush, Owl."

Sparkler was wandering the attic, skateboard under one arm. Rilla assumed he was looking for a place to spend the night.

"Guess this bed's for you," she said, then whistled to get his attention. Instantly, she realized that whistling was how one called a dog. The insulted look on Sparkler's face told her he didn't plan on coming to a dog whistle.

"Would you like a bedtime snack?" she asked, to smooth things over.

It worked. Sparkler took a pawful of chips and climbed into the drawer, snuggling down in the makeshift bed, hugging his skateboard.

Rilla tried to lift it from his arms.

"Skree-UK!"

"Okay, you can sleep with it." She patted towels around him. "Good night, little Spark."

His eyes flew open, giving her a suspicious glare.

"All right, I'll leave you alone."

Rilla backed away. Maybe tomorrow the monsters would trust her enough to let her touch them.

Now that her attic children were all tucked in, Rilla got herself ready for bed. The night was chilly. Time to put away summer nightgowns and dig out flannel pajamas. She chose ones with a verse from Revelations on the pocket: "Hurt not the earth, neither the sea nor the trees."

Climbing beneath the quilt, Rilla couldn't sleep. Puzzle pieces refused to click into place in her mind. Why had the September monster arrived alive? That hadn't happened since February—seven whole months ago! And what had sparked the other two to life the very next day?

Rilla had checked the world atlas on the wall in the classroom. Nepal and Burma and Hong Kong were located very close together. Well, close enough to touch each country with three fingers of one hand.

Did that mean the same star patterns affected the three countries at the same time? Had the stars lined up like lightning over Burma, bringing Owl to life? Then it took an extra day for the light to travel west to Nepal and east to Hong Kong? *Mmm.*

Rilla wished the Legend of the Global Monsters was as logical as math. Then she could simply create a pie chart showing when each monster would spring to life. She closed her eyes and pictured the chart:

Designing pie charts in her mind did not lull her to sleep. Now the Internet beckoned her. Maybe in the last hour, Mr. Tamerow had written. After all, when it was night here, it was morning in Finland. Mr. T. always rose at the crack of dawn. Maybe he was e-mailing her this very minute!

Rilla kicked off the quilt and hopped out of bed. Sparkler made a scared whimper, as if jolted out of a monster dream.

"Sorry, Spark," Rilla mumbled.

Feeling her way in the dark, she clicked on the computer, waiting for it to do its song and dance and deliver her to the threshold of cyberspace.

A blinking mailbox!

Not from Mr. T., but from LAF Inc.!

Gulp.

Rilla's heart thumped as she clicked on the message from CoPrez (the company president?):

We've made a connection which might be of interest to you. We will keep you posted. Soon as we have news, you'll be the first to know.

"Ho, boy." Rilla shut off the computer and hurried back to the warmth beneath the quilt. *As soon as we have news, you'll be the first to know.*

Had LAF Inc. actually found one David Charles Pinowski?

The directions in the LAF folder stated that results came faster when the persons being searched for had already filed their names with the company. Meaning, her father might be looking for her—or hoping she was looking for him.

The thought scared and delighted her so equally, she lay awake for hours before sleep erased the wild anticipation bouncing off the walls of her mind.

16

The Ultimate Love Song

"Peas, please." Rilla raised her voice to be heard above the noisy chattering at the Earth dinner table.

José, fresh from the airport, grinned at her. "Peace, please? Does that mean you want us to hush?"

Rilla giggled at his dumb joke. Having José here was fun. His hair was pulled back in a ponytail, and he sported a new earring—a tiny walrus.

The longing gazes he and Aunt Poppy kept exchanging weren't lost on Rilla. She wondered what Sparrow thought about this whole flirting game going on between her little sister and a Harmony House guest.

Rilla tuned in and out of the dinner conversation. Having three live monsters in the attic demanded half her concentration. The other half was locked on the promising message from LAF Inc.

All of the above made it hard to sit still and eat tabouli and peas.

Should she inform Sparrow of the missing person search she'd launched? Not knowing how her mother might react made deciding what to do difficult.

After dinner, Rilla helped clear plates, then Sparrow carried her masterpiece to the table—cranberry crepes filled with walnut puree, drizzled with cranberry fruit syrup. Sugar-free, of course.

The guests applauded on cue, making Sparrow beam.

Rilla groaned. If this was the highlight of her mother's day, she was spending way too much time in the kitchen. Maybe Sparrow needed somebody to flirt with, too.

After dessert, José asked if he could try out a new song on them. Fetching his guitar, he pulled a chair away from the table and began to strum a bittersweet melody.

Sounded like a love song, Rilla decided.

José's singing voice was as smooth as Sparrow's cranberry syrup.

> *We seem to be two ships*
> *passing in the night.*

> *You're too far from my lips;*
> *too far from my sight.*
>
> *I reach to take your hand,*
> *and never let it go.*
> *Will you stay beside me?*
> *My lone heart needs to know.*

With that, José stopped singing—right in the middle of the song—and held out his hand to Aunt Poppy.

Rilla fell backward in her chair. *He's singing about her! How romantic!*

Aunt Poppy's face went shock-white, and even Sparrow's jaw fell open. The only sound in the kitchen was a teapot whistling on the stove.

"What do you think of my new song?" José asked, his syrup voice remaining calm even though he *must* have known the effect he was having on all three females.

"It's called 'Poppy's Song,'" José added. "Here's the next verse."

Pulling away his hand, he strummed a lead-in, then continued:

> *Tell me that the love I see*
> *shining in your eyes*
> *is meant for me, to have, to hold.*

Your love's the sweetest prize.

Minutes spent with you alone
are precious in my life.
My heart is yours from this day forth.
Will you be my wife?

O-MI-GOSH! HE'S PROPOSING MAR-
RIAGE.

Rilla could hardly breathe. This was soooooo
thrilling. She wanted to leap up and scream, "YES!
YES! YES!"

But, of course, this tender moment had nothing
to do with her.

Aunt Poppy was gasping for air, as though her
head had been underwater in the fish tank during
four stanzas of the most beautiful love song Rilla
had ever heard. A song written just for Poppy Harmony Earth.

Sparrow began to cry.

Rilla came out of her chair, stunned. Her
mother? Crying?

"Oh, José," Sparrow squeaked, dabbing her
eyes with the hem of her *Live in Agreement with*
Nature apron.

Then Aunt Poppy began to cry.

So Rilla joined in; she couldn't help it.

All three Earth women alternated laughing and

crying, until poor José, greatly bewildered, strummed a chord to regain their attention.

Aunt Poppy gulped a few times to compose herself. Humming the lead-in, she sang: "I'll be your wife for the rest of my life."

Rilla collapsed dramatically on the floor in mock weakness.

José laughed. "Not bad, dear Poppy," he said. "Maybe we can sing together in the future."

After that came lots of hugging and kissing and Sparrow telling José how wonderful it would be to have him in the Earth family.

José scooped Rilla up in a hug. "Hey, niece-to-be," he whispered.

"Hey, almost-uncle," Rilla whispered back. She felt ecstatic that someone special in her life might actually *stay* this time and not leave and come back, leave and come back—like Mr. Tamerow and those irksome monsters who stole her heart every time.

17

Monster Mail

After dinner, Rilla lounged on the Navajo rug beside her bed.

Tonight it had taken twenty minutes of soothing (one-sided) conversation before Butterscotch's fuzzy nose emerged from underland.

Rilla sprinkled granola cereal onto a paper plate.

The sound of falling crunchies attracted Sparkler, who must have thought they were chips. He'd zoomed to the wall on his skateboard and was turning it around to zoom back. For the 8,983,625th time. Ugh.

Across the room, Owl sat at the desk, finishing Rilla's homework.

Bless his little monster heart, she thought, even though the seed of guilt over not doing her own homework was sprouting roots.

"So then," Rilla continued in a calm voice, "my mother met my father and fell in love because he wanted to save the planet as badly as she did. They got married and took off for India in search of their own truths."

"Mrrrrrph?" asked Butterscotch, nibbling on the granola.

"Exactly what I thought," Rilla said. "What does 'searching for your own truths' actually mean?"

Sparkler inched closer.

"You can listen if you want," Rilla told him.

Carrying his skateboard across the rug, he positioned it next to them and perched on it.

"After India," Rilla continued, "they traveled to other countries, living off the land, stopping to work when they needed money."

Sparkler grabbed a pawful of granola.

"Br-l-l-l-l-l!" trilled Butterscotch, making him drop it.

He scrunched his nose, as if he thought her food was disgusting.

For a second, Sparkler's crabby expression reminded Rilla of Tina Welter. Minus the fur and floppy ears, of course.

The monsters turned their gazes back to Rilla, making her feel self-conscious. They seemed eager to hear the story of her life (sort of—she hadn't gotten up to *her* part yet).

"Then my parents discovered I was on the way. They knew I was a girl and even chose my name—which means sisterhood.

"They wanted me to be born in America, so they caught a freighter home." Rilla pulled at a loop on the Navajo rug, daydreaming about the story Sparrow had told her three months ago. Every word of the tale was ingrained in Rilla's memory.

She was silent so long, Sparkler jabbed her with a paw.

"Oh, well, I'd like to say they sailed home, settled down at Harmony House, brought me into the world, and lived happily ever after."

"Moooph?" asked Butterscotch.

"No, that's not what happened."

Both monsters whimpered in disappointment.

Rilla felt pleased. More than pleased. At that moment, she wanted to hug Sparkler and Butterscotch. And Owl, too. Her own little monster family, who cared about the story of her life.

"According to my mother, somewhere in Morocco, they realized they'd married too soon, too young, and it wouldn't last. After they returned home, stopped living as nomads, and settled down, the mystique of their unique life faded away. Then my father went off to continue his search alone."

Purple monster tears soaked the fur beneath Butterscotch's eyes. Rilla's sentiments exactly. Except she'd already cried a million tears over Sparrow's missing-father story.

"After that, I was born. Three years later, my mom and her sister changed their names from Donna and Sally to Sparrow and Poppy, *and* changed our last name from Pinowski to Earth. Any effort my father might have made to find me would've been . . . well . . . difficult."

Rilla paused to sigh—something she did a lot whenever she thought about her parents' story.

"We moved several times, finally settling here. After Sparrow told me all this, I vowed to search for my father instead of waiting for him to find me."

Rilla thought about the day in June when Sparrow told her all this and gave her an envelope full of pictures and mementos belonging to her father.

"Would you like to see a picture of my father?"

The jabbery answers meant yes, Rilla assumed.

As she started to get up, a paw came down on her shoulder.

Owl handed her the envelope.

Surprised, Rilla took it. "How'd you find this?" She narrowed her eyes at him. "Were you going through my personal stuff?"

"Looking for snacks," he answered, wide-eyed and innocent.

Rilla noticed the flap had been nibbled away.

Dismayed, she pouted at Owl. "Did you eat the only pictures I have of my father?"

Before he could answer, she looked inside. Everything was there. Did Owl have a conscience? Did he know this was important stuff?

"Tasted bitter," he said. "I prefer paper with writing on it."

"Good." She was thankful he didn't eat photographs.

Rilla spread pictures and other items along the edge of the rug while the monsters discussed them amongst themselves. Owl switched to monster lingo, so Rilla didn't know what he was saying.

Butterscotch snatched up a peace symbol on a leather strap and slung it around her neck. The metal circle dangled to the floor.

Picking up a picture of her parents, Rilla studied it. Sparrow's long hair was the same, but that was all. Her face was younger, thinner, more carefree, not creased in permanent worry as it was now.

Her father was tall, but not as tall as Mr. Tamerow. He was dressed in typical end-of-the-seventies clothes, and had longish hair and a beard.

Rilla wondered what he looked like today. Sparrow had changed; certainly he'd changed, too. She tried to picture him in a suit and tie, carrying a briefcase, like Marcia Ruiz's father.

Looking at the pictures gave Rilla a sudden urge

to check her e-mail—just in case the follow-up message from LAF Inc. had arrived.

Leaving everything on the rug, she moved to the desk. Owl had faithfully printed out her homework assignment and blanked the screen. Calling up the Internet, she clicked the mouse on her blinking mailbox.

Nothing from LAF Inc.

Nothing from ABETAM.

But there were messages. Lots of them. From: **MiniMonster, MonsterBike, Monster99, LoveMonster, MonsterABC, BOYMONSTER, ImaMonster, MonsterRed,** and a half dozen other variations of the word.

"Ow-wul."

He hurried over to check "his" mail, saying something she didn't understand.

But Rilla had no reason to check all the monster messages. She knew exactly what each one said: **No, I am not a real monster.**

What if Owl's messages filled up her mailbox, leaving no room for mail from anyone else? Important mail intended for her? Sighing, she deleted the messages one by one—in spite of Owl's squawking.

The last message was from **SkateBoard.** "Spark! Not you, too. . . ."

Rilla opened the letter: **No, I am not a monster. What a stupid question.**

Click—delete.

"Why isn't Mr. Tamerow answering my mail?" she grumped, knocking on the computer screen. "He must be *really* busy in Finland."

Before signing off, Rilla zipped him a **Hi, how are you?** message. Then she added: **I have "earthshaking" news. Aunt Poppy and José are engaged!!!**

Rilla started to click on "Send," then paused. Maybe she should tease Mr. Tamerow with the earthshaking-news part and entice him to write back.

She changed the last sentence to: **e-mail me if you want to know!**

Surely he couldn't resist writing back to find out what had happened.

As Rilla packed away her envelope full of father mementos, the monsters headed off to bed. She let Butterscotch keep the peace symbol.

Too sleepy to go over the homework Owl had done, or read the assigned chapter in history, "Life in Medieval Times," she put it off till later and climbed into bed.

Thank heavens for Owl and his "all you can eat" brains.

18

Suspicions

Rilla sat alone in the classroom taking the first exam of the semester while Sparrow checked out B & B guests and collected keys. Breakfast rush was over. Now was quiet time at Harmony House.

She tapped her pencil on the math test, glad to be on the last question. This time, she'd remembered to study the review sheet after Owl filled in the answers. Too bad *she* couldn't eat her geometry book a chapter at a time and score an A.

10. Name the following geometric figures.

Under the first shape, Rilla printed *trapezoid,* hoping she'd spelled it correctly. Then, *sphere, quadrilateral, parallelogram,* and—

"May we come in?"

Aunt Poppy and José hunched guiltily in the doorway, holding hands.

"Sure."

"We know you're taking a test," Aunt Poppy whispered, "but José bought a computer wedding planner and we're eager to try it."

Rilla motioned them in. *A wedding planner? After four trips down the aisle, seems like Aunt Poppy could plan a wedding in her sleep.*

Rilla did not verbalize her thoughts, and, in fact, had to swallow three times to keep from laughing. Maybe the trick to making a marriage last was planning it on a computer.

What will they think of next? Weddings online?

Rilla watched Aunt Poppy and José tiptoe to the computer, whispering to each other, as if the tiptoeing and whispering would make them invisible.

Sparrow burst into the room, carrying a stack of teacher notebooks. "Finished?"

"Almost," Rilla answered, returning her attention to the test.

Sparrow frowned at the engaged intruders. "Are they disturbing you?"

"No." Rilla wondered if her back-to-basics mother would approve of a computer wedding planner. Quickly scribbling *pyramid* and *cone* under the appropriate figures, she handed in her test.

Sparrow put on her reading glasses and studied the paper much longer than necessary to check answers.

Something about the way she peered at the test made Rilla nervous.

"Fine," Sparrow said at last, filing the paper in her geometry folder.

Next she opened the language arts notebook. "About your *Beowulf* essay on 'Why Twentieth-Century Students Still Study a Poem from the Eighth Century' . . ."

"Yes?" Rilla held her breath, feeling defensive. She thought Owl had done a great job. Of course, what *she* thought didn't matter.

Sparrow sipped tea from a mug that read *Imagine* in fancy letters. "It's . . . well, the essay is quite good," she said. "But I expected you to go into detail about Beowulf as a static literary character who doesn't evolve emotionally. Instead, you angled your essay from the viewpoint of the monster. Interesting. Never would've thought of doing it that way."

Rilla tried so hard not to react, her lips quivered. *Owl* would think of doing it that way.

Sparrow flipped a page. "I especially liked your touching description of the monster and his relationship with his mother."

The monster and his mother. Ha! I am the monster's mother.

"This is an excellent discussion of the topic, Rill, but . . ."

Uh-oh.

"Once again, this isn't your handwriting." Sparrow looked her straight in the eye. "Explain, please?"

The seed of guilt was now a full-grown bush. A bush of guilt. If only Owl had *typed* the essay. "Like I told you," Rilla stammered, "I was just experimenting with different handwriting."

"Then why didn't you write this way on the test you just took?"

Bingo.

"Well, um, I was under exam pressure. How can I work geometry problems and change my handwriting at the same time?"

Sparrow nodded as if the answer sounded logical.

Afternoon sun slanted across the table, making Rilla glance at the earth clock. "Class dismissed?" she asked.

"Mmm." Sparrow consulted her syllabus. "Did you turn in the research assignment on materials needed for the hydroponics experiment?"

"Oh." Rilla fumbled through her notebook to find the report Owl had typed (whew!) after eating a copy of *How to Set Up a Hydroponics Lab.*

She handed the paper to Sparrow, then headed for the computer to see how the whispered wedding consultation was progressing.

"Wait," her mom ordered.

Rilla twirled, heart catching in her throat. Could Sparrow tell paws had typed the report instead of fingers? Was she that good?

"Last night, a family in the suite beneath the attic complained about someone above them Roller-blading."

Oops. Sparkler and his skateboard.

Sparrow tsk-sighed. "You know better than that, Rill. Take your Rollerblades outside from now on. Got it?"

"Got it," she answered, thankful the complaint hadn't come while she was downstairs. How could she possibly explain strange noises in the attic when she wasn't even there?

#
A Date!

Rilla headed for the attic. How could she silence Sparkler? It made sense for the July monster to be "fond of loud noises," which was clearly stated on his birth announcement.

As she hurried through the kitchen, a brightly colored box on the table caught her eye. *Cosmetics Sampler.* A note was attached:

> *This came with the wedding planner—*
> *take if you want.*
>
> *Aunt P.*

Since her all-natural mother and aunt didn't wear makeup, she might as well experiment with it. "Nifty," Rilla said, snatching it up.

"Psst!" came a voice from the back door.

Rilla whirled.

Andrew was peeking into the kitchen. "Hel-l-l-l-oooo."

What was *he* doing here?

"Will you go out with me?" he blurted.

Rilla hopped back in astonishment, catching hold of the table to steady herself. That was the *last* thing she expected him to say. "I—I—"

"Let's go see *Home for Howloween*," Andrew said, stepping inside. "The after-school matinee starts in a half hour. We can ride our bikes."

"You mean . . . right now?" Rilla was astounded and intrigued by his invitation, but she had important things to do—like check her e-mail and solve Sparkler's skateboarding dilemma.

"Why, Andrew," Sparrow said, popping into the kitchen, "what are you doing here?"

"I, um, came to take Rilla to the movies." Standing up straight, Andrew smiled his best mother-pleasing grin. "I'm even buying her ticket." He patted his pocket to let them know he had money.

"Oh, a date!" Sparrow exclaimed.

Rilla cringed. Why did mothers always say embarrassing things?

Sparrow smirked, obviously quite amused. "Rill, you didn't tell me."

Before Rilla could say *"How could I tell you if I didn't know?"* her mother added, "Run upstairs and grab a jacket first. I carried clay pots to the greenhouse at lunch, and it's freezing outside."

Andrew waited for Rilla to accept his invitation. What was she supposed to say? *Home for Howloween* was a movie she wanted to see, but . . . on a date with Andrew? *Whoa.*

"Be right back, I guess." Flying upstairs, she wondered if she would have said yes if Sparrow hadn't intercepted the invitation for her.

All was quiet in monster land. Except for snores emanating from among the stuffed animals on the pillow (Owl), from under the bed (Butterscotch), and from the bottom dresser drawer (Sparkler).

One of the best things about live monsters was afternoon nap time.

Rilla tiptoed to the computer and clicked her way onto the Internet. While waiting for the connection, she grabbed her jacket, then climbed onto a chair to reach the top shelf of her closet.

Pulling down a long box, she blew off the dust. *Shuffleboard,* the box read. A game she hadn't played in years.

Hopping off the chair, Rilla opened the lid and took out the rolled-up shuffleboard mat. Moving from one end of the bedroom to the other, she spread it out—a long, smooth pathway with no bumps. A perfect surface for a mini-skateboard. No more *click-clacking* across the hardwood floor.

"Earth, you're a genius," Rilla muttered. Tiptoe-ing to the dresser, she gently lifted the skateboard from the arms of the napping July monster. He grumble-snored, but stayed asleep.

Rilla set the skateboard at one end of the shuffle-board mat so Sparkler would get the hint when he woke up.

Then she checked her e-mail.

One message, but not from ABETAM or LAF Inc.

The letter was from **Katnip.** "Yay!" Rilla cheered, pleased to hear from her new cyber-friend. She clicked on the message:

MY CATS ARE *NOT* MONSTERS!!!! HOW CAN YOU SAY SUCH A MEAN THING? I DON'T LIKE YOU ANYMORE. DO *NOT* E-MAIL ME AGAIN! :(:(:(

"Oh, gee." The "shouted" message made Rilla feel like crying. So much for new friends. She stuck her tongue out at the three unhappy faces on the screen. "Thanks a bunch, Owl."

Rilla pouted while she put on her jacket and headed for the door. Pouting always made her feel so much better.

Wait. . . . She hesitated, one hand on the door-knob. *Earth to Earth! What are you doing?*

You're about to go to a movie—alone with a boy who's going to pay.

THIS IS YOUR FIRST DATE! ACT ACCORD-INGLY!

Mmm. Shouldn't she feel more . . . well, *excited?*

(I would if Andrew were Joshua Banks.)

Or be wearing nicer clothes?

(We're riding bikes; I'm not going to put on a dress.)

Or have fancier hair and a bit of lip gloss?

(That's reasonable.)

Rilla stepped into the tiny bathroom, brushed her hair (and teeth, just in case), then ripped open the cosmetic sampler. Blusher on both cheeks. A bit of mascara and lip gloss. Not too much, or Sparrow might march her back upstairs and make her scrub it off.

Admiring herself in the mirror, Rilla tried to muster up a bit of excitement before hurrying downstairs in anticipation of her very first date.

With a *friend* who was beginning to act like a *boyfriend.*

Go figure.

Cats, Movies, Maps, and . . . a Letter

Rilla pedaled her bike down the alley, hopping off to walk it across the lawn. Opening the barn door, she pushed the bike inside and parked it.

Dorito and Pepsi, coiled together in a furry knot, napped against a bag of crunchies, as if waiting for Rilla to sprinkle some into their bowls.

"Hey, junk-food cats. I fed you this morning."

Taco wasn't there. Rilla figured Joshua had taken him to the park, which he still did after school even though Taco was now free to play in Harmony House's generous backyard.

Oreo wound her way through a forest of rakes, hoes, and shovels. Rilla scooped up the mama cat and settled onto the bench of Aunt Poppy's weight-lifting machine. The kittens immediately sprang to life and joined her.

"Have I been ignoring you?" she cooed. "That's what happens when monsters come into my life. They demand all my attention, and I don't have time for my kitties."

Finally Milk Dud appeared in the loft. When he saw what he was missing, he leaped to the top of the cabinet, onto the Ride-a-Mower, the straw-covered floor, then scampered to Rilla for attention.

"*Home for Howloween* was good," she told them, "but scary. When it got *real* scary, Andrew held my hand. And guess what? I let him."

Rilla paused, remembering how surprised she'd been when Andrew grabbed her hand. After the scary part was over, she'd pulled away, but he held on tight.

Rilla wasn't sure how she felt about holding hands with Andrew Hogan. She only hoped Joshua didn't find out—not that he was her boyfriend or anything, but still, Joshua was . . . well, *Joshua.*

All in all, the afternoon hadn't been so bad. Andrew even told her a dumb geometry joke she hoped to try later on Sparrow:

How did the girl score an A in geometry without ever studying?

She knew all the angles.

A groaner, for sure.

Rilla wanted to linger in the barn until Joshua returned with Taco, but she didn't want to bug

Sparrow by being late for dinner, especially when they had a guest—even though it was only José.

If she hurried, she could run upstairs and check on the monsters before dinner. Kissing each cat good-bye, she jogged to the house.

"Hold it," ordered Aunt Poppy as Rilla crossed the kitchen. "Your mother is looking for you."

Something about her aunt's voice made Rilla nervous.

Aunt Poppy shut off a dinging oven timer. "She's busy with a check-in, but I'll tell her you're back from the movie. Dinner will be ready in a minute."

José zoomed into the kitchen carrying empty hors d'oeuvre trays. How quickly he'd been put to work at Harmony House, Rilla thought.

"How was your big date?" he teased.

Rilla felt herself turning twelve shades of pink. "The movie was fine," she answered, refusing to acknowledge his reference to "big date."

"Did he try to kiss you?" José pretend-frowned. "As your uncle-to-be, I have to protect you."

"Oh, geez." Rilla giggled at his feigned concern, then dashed upstairs.

In the attic, colored paper littered the floor. Rilla pieced it together. Owl had snacked on her atlas. Great. Now half of Europe was gone.

He was at the computer playing a game with

Sparkler. Monsters who played nicely together, she liked. "Where's Butterscotch?"

"The northern hemisphere," Owl answered.

Eating the atlas made him an expert in geography? "Can you narrow that down, please?"

"Bathroom."

Normally, Rilla wouldn't think anything about Butterscotch being in the bathroom. Monsters *were* "housebroken" and *did* have good hygiene habits. But the loud humming made her curious. She peeked in to see what the monster was doing.

Butterscotch balanced on the sink in front of the mirror, trying out the cosmetic sampler. Fur on her face was goopy with makeup. Her fuzzy lips were red; black eyebrows arched above each eye.

Rilla didn't know whether to laugh or strangle her. Maybe throwing her into the washing machine was a better solution.

Ignoring monster yowls, Rilla confiscated the makeup. Grabbing a washcloth, she squooshed soap and water through it, then scrubbed Butterscotch's face.

Butter shoved the cloth away and gasped for air. Shaking a paw, she gave Rilla a piece of her monster mind. Then she marched from the bathroom in a huff and disappeared beneath the bed.

"I don't have time for this," Rilla muttered. She stored the cosmetics in the cabinet and hurried to her desk. "May I borrow my computer, please? Emphasis on *my*."

Reluctantly, Owl and Sparkler stopped the game and moved aside while Rilla connected to the Internet.

A blinking mailbox. Ho-hum.

Rilla didn't bother to get excited—or even sit down. Instead, she braced herself for an annoying list of messages from "monster this" and "monster that."

But there was only one message.

And it wasn't from a monster at all.

It was from somebody named:

DCPinowski. . . .

21
The Message

Rilla stared at the screen until **DCPinowski** lasered a beam through her eyes into her brain. Into that cookie tin inside her mind where all those hopes and fears about her father were neatly packed away.

Owl and Sparkler watched her with cocked heads and puzzled expressions.

Rilla sank into the chair. How many DCPinowskis could there possibly be in cyberspace?

Owl poked her. "You got mail."

Rilla glanced at him. Was his understatement intentional? Or was he in a hurry to get back to his game?

"Remember the story I told you about my father?" Rilla began. "Who I've never seen or met or talked to?"

Owl studied her so intently through his thick

glasses, he appeared to be reading her mind. Sparkler made a sympathetic chortling sound. Even Butterscotch stuck her freshly scrubbed nose out from underland.

"This letter," Rilla told them in a raspy whisper. "It might be from him."

Owl lunged for the mouse to click open the message.

Rilla snatched it from his paw. Monsters were sooooo impatient.

"You don't understand," she said. "I've waited my whole life for this moment."

"So—open the letter," Owl urged, like it was no big deal.

Rilla stared at the screen. Variations of what the message might say flashed through her mind:

I don't have a daughter.

Or: **I'm looking for my son. Are you him?**

Then she pictured what she *hoped* to read:

Are you my Rilla? She'd be thirteen now.

And what she most feared:

Leave me alone. I don't want to know you.

"Open it!" Owl screeched, flapping his paws in exasperation.

Butterscotch scurried from beneath the bed and clambered to the desktop, bumping Sparkler out of her way so she could see the computer screen.

Rilla lunged to catch the July monster, but he flomped to the floor.

Scrambling to his paws, he chittered a string of nastiness at Butterscotch, then climbed into Rilla's lap.

The closeness of her monster family seemed like a shield against the e-mail message—just in case it wasn't friendly.

Clank, clank, clank!

Go away, Sparrow.

Go away, world.

This is more important than being on time for dinner.

"I can't do this," Rilla whispered. She scooted the mouse toward Owl. "You open it. You read it to me."

She bowed her head, prepared to listen.

Sparkler leaned back, staring up at her with woeful eyes. Butter cooed encouragement, reaching to stroke Rilla's arm, leaving a smear of leftover blusher on Rilla's sleeve.

Click-click went the mouse.

Pause.

"What does it say?" Rilla hissed, feeling as impatient as a hungry monster.

Owl began to read in his thin, cartoony voice.
" **'Dearest Rilla—'** "

"Stop!" Rilla's head snapped up. "I want to read it."

She reread the words **"Dearest Rilla,"** rolling them off her tongue in a whisper as if they were the most delicious words in the English language.

> **Is it really you? My daughter whom I've tried to find for thirteen years? Is your mother Donna Knox? My heart will break if you're not the one I've been searching for. Please answer soon. Please be my Rilla.**
>
> **David C. Pinowski**

Tears trickled down Rilla's face. And Sparkler's. *Please be my Rilla.*

Wrapping her arms around Sparkler, she let the tears come. He held still, as if he knew he shouldn't squirm at an important moment like this.

Butterscotch began to whimper. Monster tears. Tiny and purple.

Owl ripped a piece of paper from the printer and nibbled on it, as if embarrassed by everyone else's reactions.

CLANK! CLANK! CLANK!
Okay, okay.

Rilla wiped her eyes. Time for dinner. But first—
a reply.

She had tons to say to this man who was her
father. But right now she felt shy, speechless.

Maybe all she should say is yes. Yes, it's me. I
am your Rilla.

Quickly she clicked on "Reply" and typed:

Yes.

Then sent her affirmation whirling through
cyberspace.

Straight to her father's electronic mailbox—and
heart.

22

In Which earthgirl Eats Only One Bite of Dinner

Each step toward the kitchen upped the level of Rilla's angst. *I should have said more. Should have told him about myself.*

And what about mentioning Sparrow to her father? Or mentioning her father to Sparrow?

Yikes.

The kitchen felt warm and cozy. Aromas in the air announced dinner: spicy chili. Meatless, of course. With the homemade seven-seed garlic bread Aunt Poppy was lifting from the oven.

José was pouring organic apple juice into everyone's goblet. No one was talking, which tipped Rilla off that something was terribly wrong.

"There you are," Sparrow said, clattering chili bowls onto the table.

Rilla shivered in spite of the overheated kitchen,

resisting the urge to bolt out the door and move into the barn with Taco and the cats. "What's going on?"

Aunt Poppy gave her a sympathetic look as she scooped steaming bread into a wicker basket.

"Sit," Sparrow commanded.

Rilla sat.

José dished up chili from a covered Crock-Pot in the center of the table. He seemed embarrassed by the tension in the air.

Rilla studied everybody. "Wha-at?"

"I got a phone call," Sparrow began, "from the Internet company. We signed up for five hours a month, and it seems we've used up our first five hours in less than a week. And then some."

"Really?" Five hours seemed like a looooong time to be online.

Sparrow glowered at her. "Is that all you can say? Abe told me he cautioned you to watch your time online. Why are you being so careless?"

I'm not careless. It's Owl's fault. He goes crazy with e-mail the minute I leave the attic.

"Explain, please?"

"I—I guess I need to, um, watch the time when I'm online."

"Ril-la." Sparrow took the bowl José offered. "Merging onto the superhighway was *not* a good idea—in spite of what Abe said. We have to cancel."

"NO!"

Aunt Poppy and José flinched at Rilla's over-reaction.

Sparrow simply handed her a bowl of chili. "A customer service rep from the Internet company called. They make a courtesy call to all new accounts to make sure no one is having any difficulties with their service. The company rep told me that if we planned to be heavy users, she could put us under a different billing plan."

The term "heavy users" made Rilla break out in a cold sweat.

"When I asked what she meant, she explained that our first bill would be humongous—based on our present rate of usage."

Rilla gulped. *Okay, Earth, time for half-truths.*

"I, um, accidentally stayed online when I wasn't in the attic," Rilla said, trying to sound apologetic. It was partially true, yet she couldn't explain that a *monster* had caused the problem.

"So, are you going to pay the bill?" her mother asked.

Rilla squinted at the ceiling, calculating the cost of monster food plus online time. No way could she ask Joshua Banks for *that* much money. She'd have to get a full-time job to support the monsters and maintain her access to cyberspace. *Impossible.*

"I promise to be more careful."

Sparrow unfolded a linen napkin and smoothed it into her lap. "We have to disconnect the service, Rill. We simply can't afford it."

Panic tightened Rilla's throat at the thought of getting this close to her father, only to have the opportunity yanked away by the pull of a plug.

"*Please* wait. I deserve another chance—since I, um, didn't know."

Sparrow paused to sip her apple juice. "Give me one good reason why we need the Internet."

Rilla targeted Sparrow's interests instead of her own. "There's a cooking club and a gardening club—with tips on greenhouses—and—"

"I can do all those things off-line. I don't need cyberspace and neither do you."

"But I can e-mail Mr. Tamerow and José."

"You can write regular letters to Mr. Tamerow, and you won't need to write José at all because he's moving to Harmony House."

"He is?"

Rilla and José exchanged smiles. Hers was a pleased smile at the happy news. His seemed unsure. Was he having second thoughts about getting caught in the middle of future Earth family arguments?

Sparrow slurped her chili. "End of discussion. I'm canceling after dinner."

Rilla's insides turned stone cold. If Sparrow canceled that soon, it meant she'd never hear back from her father. He'd be lost to her forever. She had no idea where he lived or how to get in touch with him.

And what would *he* think when his letters came back marked **Undeliverable?**

Answering her father's message with a simple **Yes** had been stupid. *I should have told him where I live.*

Suddenly Rilla's heart felt as gray and full of tears as the gloomy September rain clouds. She began to cry. To sob.

Everyone stared, murmuring explanations for her behavior:

"She's at 'that age.' "

"She blows things way out of proportion."

"Sometimes trivial stuff upsets her."

Rilla leaped to her feet. "No! It's none of those things."

Dismayed at standing there sniffling in front of José, Rilla took a breath and wiped her eyes on her napkin. "If you disconnect us after dinner, I'll never hear back from . . . from . . ."

"From who?" Sparrow asked. "Abe?"

"No."

Say it, Earth, it's your last hope.

She locked angry gazes with her mother. "From DCPinowski."

All movement at the table froze.

Aunt Poppy choked on a bite of bread. José's spoon stopped halfway to his mouth. Sparrow's face turned as white as the kitchen walls.

"From David?" Aunt Poppy blurted as soon as she could speak. "You mean, you heard from your father?"

Sparrow made a funny squeaking sound but said nothing.

"Yes." Rilla nodded and sniffled some more.

Aunt Poppy nudged Sparrow. "Hear that, sis? She heard from David."

Sparrow seemed too stunned to respond.

Flustered, Rilla tried to explain. "I've, um, gotten only one message—just a minute ago, when I went upstairs."

Feeling drained, she sat down and ate a spoonful of chili. It was cold.

Finally, Sparrow moved, plunking her spoon onto the table. "You heard from your father?"

"Yes."

Sparrow's hands shook as she clutched a napkin. "However did you find him?" Her quiet voice was filled with awe.

Rilla told them about the LAF Inc. service she'd stumbled across her first day online.

Her mother twisted the napkin into a knot as she listened. "How do you know it's really *him*?" The mother-teacher voice sounded suspicious.

Seeing Sparrow suffer made Rilla feel remorse and pleasure at the same time—which in turn made her feel guilty. She cleared her throat. "He asked if my mother was Donna Knox."

"Oh, Lord." Sparrow took a quick swig of apple juice as if that might make the news go down easier.

"So what did he say?" Aunt Poppy urged. "What did he tell you?"

Suddenly Rilla felt she was betraying a trust. "He didn't tell me anything. We just established the fact that we were who the other had been looking for." (At least those words made sense to her.)

"Let's go upstairs and read the message." Aunt Poppy scooped chili into her mouth in a rush to finish dinner. "Let's send a group hello."

Rilla's heart leaped into a gallop. "No, please . . . I mean . . ." She couldn't let everyone tromp to the attic. The reason had nothing to do with sending her father a group hello. It had to do with three live monsters.

"Why not?" Aunt Poppy asked. "This news is almost as big as our engagement announcement." She punctuated her sentence with a sappy smile in José's direction.

José covered Aunt Poppy's hand with his. "Give Rilla a little time. She's never met her father; she needs to talk to him alone. Let her share him with the rest of the family when she's ready."

Thank you, thank you, thank you. Rilla loved José for defending her right to keep her father all to herself. For a while, at least. But the final decision would have to come from Sparrow.

Color was flushing back into her mother's cheeks. "Okay, Rill. We'll stay online a while longer. Mainly so you can talk to . . . uh . . . him. I agree with José."

Relief calmed Rilla's heart. She touched her mom's arm. "You're not mad at me for finding him?"

Sparrow sat up straight, surprised. "How could I be mad at you? He's your father. You have a right to know him." She fanned herself with her knotted napkin. "It's just such a major shock. Why didn't you tell me you were looking for him?"

"In June you told me my father had probably tried to find me. I wanted to help him. I mean, from this end."

Rilla couldn't wait to get back to the computer. "Is it all right if I tell him where we live?"

"Of course," Sparrow said, fanning faster. "I'd, uh, be curious to know where he lives, too."

Aha. Sparrow was curious.

Rilla shoved away her cold chili. "I'm not hungry. Can I go to my room and write to him?"

Her mother's face got all misty. Rilla wasn't sure she'd ever seen that expression before. "Of course," Sparrow said. "Go."

"Oh, yeah, just up and leave," José teased. "That's *much* more important than gooseberry yogurt pie for dessert."

His joke broke the tension in the kitchen.

Dessert was the *last* thing on Rilla's mind. She practically sprang from the table in her eagerness to get back to her e-mail.

"Wait," Sparrow called.

"I won't stay online long," Rilla promised. All she had to figure out was how to keep Owl *off*-line.

"That's not why I stopped you." Sparrow placed a hand over her heart. "I just want you to, uh, well, I mean . . . When you write to your father, give him my best—no, uh, just say a simple hello. No, wait . . ."

José and Aunt Poppy giggled while Sparrow stumbled for words.

"Tell him," her aunt chimed in, "that everyone in the Earth family sends their warmest greetings."

Sparrow nodded vigorously. "Yes. That's good. Tell him that."

Rilla ran up the back steps. "The only problem," she mumbled when they were out of earshot, "is that my father has no idea who on earth the Earth family is. . . ."

23

Butter in Underland

Rilla whirled and twirled, dancing a waiting-for-the-modem ballet she'd invented—something goofy to pass the time while the modem dialed the local access number and connected the attic to cyberspace.

All three monsters sprawled on the bed, playing cards with the tiny deck belonging to Sparkler.

Rilla was immensely glad these monsters played so well together. She recalled others who refused to get along, causing havoc in the attic.

Icicle and Sweetie Pie. They hated each other.

Burly and Chelsea. They squabbled like selfish toddlers.

"Welcome," said the robotic computer voice, drawing Rilla back to her desk. "You've got mail."

Wow. Had her father written back already?

No. The message was from Mr. Tamerow! Well—*fi-nal-ly*. Boy, did she have lots to tell him.

Dear Rilly,
   Sorry to be so long answering your many notes.

Good. He'd gotten her messages. She was beginning to wonder if mail from earthgirl7 had spiraled into a deep cyber well.

I've been terribly busy. I confess I did not come to Helsinki on business. I came to meet Minna. She is my e-mail buddy. We have been writing to each other for two years.

Minna? He'd never mentioned her before.
That's because you always talk about your own life, Earth, not his.
True. Now she felt guilty.

Guess what, Rilly? I GOT MARRIED!!!

"M-married?!" she stammered to the computer screen.

**I know this will surprise you. Took us
by surprise, too. But Minna and I are
very happy, and I adore the twins.**

Twins? The woman has TWINS?

**That's right, Rilly, I'm an instant
father. Aleksis and Elias. They are four
and quite a handful. I can't wait for
you to meet my new family. I am
taking leave from my job and staying
here a few months, but we plan to be
stateside for Christmas. Please share
my good news with your mother and
aunt.**

**Love to all,
the Tamerow family**

The Tamerow family. Words that pierced Rilla's
heart.

Why? You should congratulate Mr. T.

*But he has an instant family. A wife and two
kids. He'll forget me.*

He won't forget you; he knew you first.

Humph. Things will never be the same.

With movements akin to a zombie, Rilla printed
out Mr. Tamerow's message so Sparrow and Aunt
Poppy could read it for themselves. She wasn't sure

she could tell them the "good" news without sounding as though she were announcing the imminent extinction of all endangered species.

Pausing, she scanned the letter three more times, hoping she'd simply read it wrong. But the words didn't change. They still said Mr. Tamerow got married. Still said he had two kids.

Be happy. You found your father. Maybe now you won't need to depend so much on Mr. Tamerow.

Rilla clicked on "Compose Mail," wishing her happiness over finding her father didn't have to be tempered by losing Mr. Tamerow.

You didn't lose him.

Okay, okay. Sometimes her inner voice irritated her as much as Sparrow's bossy mother voice.

From: earthgirl7
To: DCPinowski

Rilla paused. *What if your father has kids, too? What if he has so many kids, he doesn't need one more?*

Rilla's hand tightened around the mouse. Could it be true? Maybe there were tons of things about her father she was better off not knowing. What if he was an awful, horrible person? What if he was so bad, he'd written to her from prison?

Yikes.

Her family's list of "Explanations for Rilla's Strange Behavior" popped into her mind. Maybe her fears *were* due to being "at that age." Maybe she *did* blow things way out of proportion, or get upset over trivial stuff.

Taking a deep breath, Rilla continued typing. For better or worse, she had to know more about her father. And she had to know if he wanted to claim her as his daughter.

I used to be Rilla Pinowski. Now I am Rilla Harmony Earth. My mother, Donna Knox Pinowski, is Sparrow Harmony Earth. Aunt Sally is now Poppy Harmony Earth, engaged to José Pacheco. We moved many times, most recently to Harmony House, a bed-and-breakfast. I am home-schooled.

What else should she tell him? How she'd thought about him her entire life? How she'd secretly wondered (at first) if her membership in the Monster of the Month Club had come from him?

Maybe those things could be said later. Maybe this was all she needed to tell him right now.

Rilla signed the letter, **your daughter,** then sent it, hoping nothing she'd told him would make him change his mind about her. After all, her message *was* kind of weird.

Rilla moved her stuffed animal collection to the rocking chair, hoping the card-playing monsters got the hint that she wanted to go to bed.

"So, guys, how do you play monster cards?" The instant she asked the question, her gaze fell upon a pile of monster belongings in the middle of the bed. Were they playing a gambling game? Winning possessions away from each other?

Rilla wasn't bothered by the sight of Butterscotch's love beads, or one of Sparkler's knee pads. What bothered her was the sight of Owl's glasses in Butter's pile of loot. Didn't Owl's selection card say "Never remove his glasses"?

Uh-oh.

Snatching them up, Rilla tried to shove them back onto Owl's face.

Butterscotch yapped at her. Ripping them from Rilla's grasp, she stashed them back in her pile.

"Fine," Rilla said. "Game's over. Time for bed."

Monster grumbles and groans and grunts.

Then, miraculously, they obeyed her. Butterscotch and Owl handed their cards to Sparkler, who stacked them neatly on top of the dresser.

Rilla gloated. *I am MonsterMom and they obey me!*

Butterscotch collected her hoard, scampering off the bed to underland before Rilla could stop her.

"Hey, Owl, she took your glasses."

Owl glared in Rilla's general direction. "She won them fair and square." Hopping off the bed, he smashed headfirst into the dresser.

Rilla covered her mouth to keep from laughing, although the collision must have hurt. Taking hold of Owl's tiny shoulders, she attempted to steer him around the bed, but he wiggled away.

After tripping on the edge of the Navajo rug and banging his head on the bedpost, he guided himself, paw over paw, to the rocker, then climbed up to burrow into the stuffed animal pile, grumbling all the way.

Rilla flopped over the side of the bed and lifted the quilt. "Hey, Butter, give me Owl's glasses. He can't see."

Faint snoring was her answer.

Rats.

Sparkler awkwardly climbed into the dresser drawer, off balance, thanks to only one knee pad.

Bummed, Rilla got ready for bed. *Just when I become thankful the monsters get along, they start to bicker.*

Clicking off the light, she settled in. More important things than monsters promised to fill her dreams.

Her father.

The Tamerow family.

Her homework. *Oops.*

"Owl?" Rilla whispered in the dark. "Did you finish my homework?"

She'd fed him math for an entree and history for dessert, but hadn't seen him working on the assignment sheets. He'd been too busy playing computer games, then monster cards.

"It'll get done," came a sleepy Owl voice.

"When?"

"It'll get *done!*" Sleepy gave way to irritable.

"Okay, okay." Sighing, Rilla closed her eyes. Guilt tried to shove her out of bed to do her own homework, but she was soooo tired.

Might as well let Owl do it one more time.

Not to worry. He'd never let her down before.

24
Beware the Warnings

The earthy smell of rich loam scented the greenhouse as the home-schoolers filled long trays with potting soil in preparation for planting.

Rilla brushed dirt from her hands, then pulled off her sweater and tied it around her waist. Outside, the wind was nippy, but inside, the air was warm and humid, thanks to the the solar collectors.

She'd barely said two words to anyone this morning, lost in her own thoughts about the events of yesterday. Disappointment at not finding a morning message in her electronic mailbox made her heart sag.

So maybe her father was working and hadn't checked his e-mail.

Even so, the worst possible reasons for not hearing from him queued up in her mind:

Prison guards limited his access to a computer.

His fourteen kids kept him too busy to respond to messages.

Her reply had been so weird, he'd decided not to answer.

Stop it, Earth.

Rilla scratched her nose with the back of her wrist to keep from smudging her face with dirt. Working her hands in the soil soothed her roller-coaster emotions. She wasn't even annoyed by Tina Welter dancing outside the greenhouse with Milk Dud instead of helping inside like she was supposed to. At least she wasn't Joshua's shadow for a change.

Mr. Tamerow's news had been the talk of the breakfast table. Sparrow and Aunt Poppy were giddy as they planned ways to welcome the new Tamerow family to America. They'd be invited to Harmony House for Christmas, which coincided with the Earth-Pacheco wedding, scheduled for Christmas Eve in the parlor.

Rilla admitted to catching a smidgen of their excitement. How could she not? Aunt Poppy's enthusiasm was contagious. Plus, she couldn't wait to see Harmony House lavishly decorated for the holiday wedding. She knew the creative Earth sisters would do it up real fancy.

After that, breakfast table conversation switched

to the topic of Rilla's father. Yes, she'd written to tell him of the name changes and the various moves. No, she hadn't heard back.

"Rilla!" hollered Mrs. Welter, rudely interrupting her daydreams. "Andrew and Wally are ready to treat the water for the hydroponic experiment. Do you want to come watch?"

"Oh, yes," she called back. "More than anything in the world."

Mrs. Welter shot her a "Don't get sassy" look, but said nothing. The "Rilla found her father" news had spread among the home-schoolers faster than Sparkler's skateboard could zip across the attic floor.

Everyone was being overly patient and nice. Joshua kept giving her sympathetic smiles, and Andrew kept winking, as though she and he shared a special secret—which, in a way, they did.

Wiping her dirty hands on her jeans, Rilla plodded to the project corner while Mrs. Welter rounded up the others. Joshua and Marcia had been outside sorting packets of seeds, deciding what to plant.

As the group gathered inside the greenhouse, Joshua and Andrew kept their distance from each other, which amused Rilla.

Tina carried in Milk Dud, with Taco nipping at her heels. Even she had stopped her snide remarks.

Rilla only wished Tina would leave Milk Dud alone.
Hands off. He's an Earth cat; he belongs to me.

Rilla watched Wally and Andrew add the necessary nutrients to the water and suspend the plant roots from specially designed holders. Now all they had to do was take weekly notes on the progress.

Next, the home-schoolers gathered in the classroom to go over their homework assignment since it was too cold to sit on the patio.

Andrew's mother had sent Australian treats called wallaby cakes to munch on. Even though the name sounded exotic, they were simply cookie bars cut in the shape of kangaroos.

Mrs. Welter bit the head off a wallaby, then dabbed at her perfect lipstick with the corner of a napkin. "Let's go over your history homework. Life in the fifteenth century."

Papers shuffled and binders snapped open and shut as everyone fetched worksheets. Rilla was grateful to Owl for rising at the crack of dawn to fill in the answers. He'd kept his word. He was a good little monster.

"Exchange papers with the person next to you," Mrs. Welter ordered.

More shuffling. Rilla exchanged with Wally.

"Number one," Mrs. Welter began. "How many centuries have passed since *Beowulf* was written?"

"Seven," Marcia said.

"Good," exclaimed Mrs. Welter.

Rilla marked Wally's answer correct.

Wally snickered.

"What is it?" asked Mrs. Welter.

Wally gave Rilla an "Are you crazy?" kind of look.

Uh-oh. In the morning rush, she'd snatched her worksheet from Owl's paw and shoved it into her history folder with nary a glance.

Wally cleared his throat, acting important. "Rilla's answer is 14,110."

Everyone laughed.

Rilla heated up. Where had she heard that number before? She closed her eyes. The Pikes Peak booklet! The elevation of Pikes Peak is 14,110 feet. Owl had used correct information—but not information that matched the question.

She grabbed for her paper.

Wally yanked it away and held it from her reach. "And, and." He laughed. "Number two. Name four types of weapons used to defend castles in medieval times. Rilla's answer is 'Transistors, frame, knobs, and printed circuit boards.'"

Owl had named four parts of a radio!

Mortified, Rilla dipped her head, letting hair hide her blushing face. Laughter and teasing stung her ears. So *that's* what happens when the monster's glasses are removed.

Beware the warnings. . . .

Rilla's mind whipped into action. There was only one thing to do—milk everyone's sympathy. Make them think she'd cracked over the missing-father issue.

Leaping from her chair, she ripped the paper from Wally's hand and bolted from the classroom. No one called her back or hurried after her.

She made a beeline for the attic—immensely grateful Sparrow hadn't been there to witness her staged breakdown.

For once, angst had worked in her favor.

25

A Gambling Game

When Rilla arrived in the attic, Owl was at the computer. She knew he wasn't online since she'd unplugged the modem earlier to prevent him from cruising cyberspace.

Sparkler and Butterscotch sat in the middle of the rug, playing monster cards. July appeared to be losing all his toys to August, one by one.

Rilla flopped her history worksheet onto the desk in front of Owl. "All these answers are wrong," she huffed.

Without glasses, Owl had to hold the paper to his nose to read it. "These are *good* answers."

Rilla scoffed. "Good answers to wrong questions." Whirling, she stalked toward the card game. "Butter. Give back Owl's glasses. Now."

All three monsters began squawking at once.

"Hold it. Hold it." Rilla made a time-out sign like an umpire. "I need an interpreter. Owl, explain please?" (Now she sounded like Sparrow.)

Owl didn't bother to look at her since he couldn't see her anyway. "I can't get my glasses back unless I *win* them back. It's the rule. And Butter wins almost every hand. She must have had a lot of gambling time on her paws in Nepal."

Rilla whisked Owl off the chair and deposited him on the rug.

"Hey, watch it!" he sputtered, straightening his cap.

"Play," she commanded. "Deal him in, Butter. He has to win his glasses back."

Butterscotch gave a challenging chortle and dealt the cards. Picking Owl's glasses from her winning stash, she set them in the bidding pile.

Owl removed his cap and tassel and tossed them into the ring.

They waited for Sparkler to search through every pocket in his jeans, but Butterscotch had already won all his toys.

Smugly, she reached for his skateboard.

"Scree-UK!" Sparkler bounded to his feet and yanked the board away.

"He's not going to part with his skateboard," Rilla interpreted. She wished Owl had been that attached to his glasses.

Without missing a beat, Butterscotch picked up Sparkler's cards, shuffled them into the deck, and dealt two hands.

Rilla pointed a chewed-off nail at Owl. "Win," she ordered.

No need to hover over the card game. She might make Owl nervous. Returning to the computer, Rilla crawled under the desk, plugged in the modem, and signed onto the Internet. Holding her breath, she clicked on the blinking mailbox.

Seeing the name **DCPinowski** almost stopped Rilla's heart.

This is it, Earth. Time to find out who he is and where he is.

Yikes, yikes, yikes, yikes, yikes.

Rilla fumbled with the mouse. Her nerves were so shredded, she could hardly get it positioned to click on the message.

Leaning back in her chair, she hugged herself for comfort as she read, finally, the long-awaited message from her father:

Hearing from you is about the best thing that's ever happened to me. There's so much I want to tell you. And ask you. Thanks for the news about moving and the name change. That explains why you and Donna seemed

to disappear off the face of the earth. (No pun intended.)

Ha. He's funny—like José.

Sparrow. That touched my heart. Sparrow is the nickname I gave Donna when we met. Your mother reminded me of a dainty bird, always in flight.

Rilla gulped. Wow. Sparrow never explained how she'd chosen her name. Knowing the nickname had come from her father made Rilla feel connected to him. She read on:

I live in Oregon and work as a forest ranger at Crater Lake National Park.

I knew he had to work close to nature.

To put the past thirteen years into a nutshell, after your mom and I separated, I joined the Peace Corps and worked in Zimbabwe for three years. Came home for a year and tried to find you.

When I failed, I signed up for another stint with the Peace Corps, this time in Botswana.

Botswana! That's where Icicle, the January monster, had come from. Rilla knew lots about Botswana. Maybe someday she could impress her father with conversations about South African animals, like klipspringers, lesser bush babies, or vervet monkeys.

When I returned to the States, I went to college, married again, then divorced. No kids. After that, I wandered here and there, finally landing in Oregon, where I live and work in the wilderness.

I never stopped looking for you, Rilla. My heart's desire is to come and visit. If you (or Donna) nix this plan, I will understand. But if it's possible, just say when. After November, I will have a week's vacation.

Rilla began to hyperventilate.

This was too much to take in. In a matter of seconds, all her questions had been answered. Well, most of them. And he wanted to come visit—holy smokes! The prospect of actually meeting him thrilled her. But it also meant he and Sparrow would have to come face to face again. . . .

Suddenly this whole event had gotten complicated—too big for her to handle alone. Sparrow would have to be in on this.

Rilla printed out her father's letter.

Time to head downstairs for another mother-daughter talk.

Only this time *she* had the missing-father answers.

26

Bartering
with Butter

As Rilla rose from her desk, commotion on the rug stopped her.

Oops. She'd forgotten about the monster card game.

Butterscotch's stash of winnings was piled even higher.

Owl had lost everything. He was down to his underwear.

"Hey," Rilla yelped. "You can't take his clothes."

Butterscotch snipped back an answer that sounded like, "Ohhh, yes I can."

Groaning, Rilla knelt on the floor and tried to reason with her—in English.

Owl kept quiet, as if he knew reasoning with August monsters was impossible.

| 155 |

Rilla's gaze landed on her father's peace symbol, still hanging around Butterscotch's neck. It gave her an idea. She reached to remove it.

The monster's paws frantically clutched the strap.

Rilla held on. Aha. Butter wasn't going to give up her peace symbol any more than Spark would gamble away his skateboard.

"This belongs to me," Rilla said in her best Mrs.-Welter-calm-and-patient voice. "You didn't win it. I lent it to you."

Butter fussed, nipping at Rilla's hand.

Startled, Rilla jerked away. "You bit me!"

Owl snickered.

"What are *you* laughing at? If I hadn't stopped the game, you'd be sitting here naked."

An insulted Owl spun his back to her.

"Look, Butter. I'll let you keep the peace symbol. On one condition."

"Mummpth?"

"You trade Owl's glasses for it."

"Mipplenop," Butter jeered.

Rilla grabbed the leather strap.

"Yeeeep!"

"Well? *My* game has rules, too."

Big monster sigh. Butterscotch lifted the glasses from her stash as if they were a monster heirloom. Reluctantly, she handed them to Owl.

The instant Owl put them on, he reacted to the fact that he was sitting on the rug in his undies. Scrambling to his feet, he raced for the bathroom.

Rilla fetched her jewelry box from the top of the dresser. Butterscotch practically climbed on top, trying to pry it open.

"Wait." Rilla peeked inside, drawing out a button bracelet she'd made in kindergarten. "I'll trade you this for Owl's pants."

Butterscotch lunged for the bracelet.

Rilla yanked it away.

Grumping, the monster grabbed Owl's pants, waddled to the bathroom, and flung them inside.

Rilla could hear Owl zipping them up.

"I'll trade you this for Owl's cape." Rilla held up one of the sand dollars Mr. Tamerow had sent from Greece.

The trade was made. And on it went until Rilla had bartered back all of Owl's and Sparkler's possessions.

A delighted Butterscotch scurried beneath the bed with her new loot. Rilla didn't mind giving her own possessions to the monster. Wasn't like they'd be taken from the attic; they still belonged to her.

Sparkler stuffed toys back into his pockets.

Owl marched from the bathroom, fully clothed, his ego shot down a notch or two. He headed for the computer. Rilla beat him there, unplugging the modem. On second thought, she unhooked the cord and removed the entire thing to keep him from plugging it back in and going online.

She was smarter than the average monster. . . .

Retrieving the letter from her father, Rilla headed downstairs, leaving the modem hidden in the dim attic stairwell.

Aunt Poppy was tidying up after the B & B guests finished the hors d'oeuvres. Sparrow sat at the table, peeling and chopping organic carrots. José sat next to her, making a list of guests to invite to the wedding.

Rilla's brain flashed back to the day Aunt Poppy was lounging on the patio, secretly making lists in a notebook. So that was it. She'd had wedding plans on her mind long before José popped the question.

Pausing, Rilla felt unsure about sharing her father's letter in front of the entire family.

José stopped writing to glance up at her. "How are you feeling?"

Everyone studied her with furrowed brows. Ah, they'd heard about her "breakdown" during history class.

"I'm fine," she said, sitting at the table and nabbing a carrot coin to munch.

Sparrow reached to straighten her daughter's bangs. "If you need to talk about anything, it's okay. We're here to listen."

"Well . . . I have news. From my father."

Sparrow gave a little gasp, dropped the carrot peeler, and wiped her hands on a towel. "Let me see."

"No," said Aunt Poppy. "Read the letter out loud so everyone can hear."

Rilla glanced at her mother. "Is it all right?"

Emotion twisted Sparrow's face. Was she afraid of what the letter might say? Leaving the table with an abruptness that knocked her chair against the cabinets, she retreated to the sink, turning her back to them. "Okay, go ahead. Read the letter."

So Rilla did. Her voice shook during the mushy parts, like "Your mother reminded me of a dainty bird, always in flight."

When Rilla finished, tension in the kitchen evaporated.

"Oh, that's so sweet," Aunt Poppy cooed in a quiet voice.

"He seems like a really decent guy," José added.

Sparrow sniffled.

Rilla scooted from the table to put her hand on her mother's shoulder.

Turning, Sparrow hugged her. "Sorry," she whispered. "I didn't mean to let this affect me. It's just been so long since I heard from . . . Well, I'm glad to know he's all right."

Sparrow's reaction pleased Rilla immensely. So.

Her mother had been concerned. For thirteen years? Then why didn't *she* try to find him?

"Why didn't you try to find him?" The words leaped from Rilla's mouth before she could stop them.

Sparrow wiped her eyes. "I did."

"You did?" This came from Aunt Poppy and José as well as Rilla.

"His news about the Peace Corps explains why my letters were returned. I didn't know he joined, although we'd talked about it. I figured he'd disappeared so I couldn't find him. I stopped trying after a couple of years, but it was hard for me to believe he didn't want to meet his own daughter."

She touched Rilla's cheek. "Thanks for doing this. Now I can put all those questions to rest and get on with my life."

Aunt Poppy tapped a finger on José's notebook. "Add David Pinowski's name to our guest list."

"What?!" Rilla's voice rose three octaves. "You mean you're inviting him to your wedding?"

"And Christmas," Aunt Poppy added. "Is it okay, sis?"

Sparrow's face paled. Rilla had a hard time reading it, although "panic" seemed like a good description.

Quiet filled the kitchen. What was going through her mother's mind?

Acting self-conscious, Sparrow returned to the table. "David and Rilla have to meet sometime. He said he couldn't come till after November, so Christmas would be perfect."

Sitting up straight, Sparrow sucked in her stomach. "Besides, it gives me a few months to prepare for the trauma of seeing my ex-husband again."

Everyone laughed—but not Rilla. This was too important for frivolity.

One of her lifelong dreams was finally coming true. Spending Christmas with her father. And her mother. Like a real family.

Well, *almost* like a real family.

Most families don't include monsters.

27

Freeze!

Rilla straightened the quilt and snuggled against the pillows. Notebooks surrounded her. She'd climbed into bed way early to do her homework, even though it was Friday night and she didn't have to worry about school for a couple of days.

After the history class fiasco and the return of Owl's glasses, all in monster-land did not return to normal. The removal of Owl's glasses had permanently disabled his ability to "eat and remember."

Rilla had figured this out immediately after she saw Owl's answer to question number one on tonight's science worksheet: *hot dogs, chips, and apple pie.*

Unfortunately, the question wasn't: *Name the July monster's food.* It was: *Name three nutrients added to water to sustain the life and growth of plants in our hydroponics project.*

Erasing Owl's answer, Rilla looked it up herself and wrote: *potassium nitrate, calcium sulfate, and monocalcium phosphate.*

"Back to doing my own homework," she grumbled, knowing all along the monster homework machine was too good to last. At least now her guilt was eased.

Beyond the half-circle of notebooks sat her monster children, playing cards and placing bids—only this time with coins from Rilla's panda bank instead of personal possessions.

Now the games could end in peace.

R-i-i-i-ng-g-g-g!

"One, two, three, four, five," counted Rilla.

Clank, clank, clank.

The call was for her.

Scrambling from bed, she hurried down to the third-floor landing and snatched up the guests' cordless phone. "Hello?"

It was her one true love.

Rilla carried the phone back to the attic, filling Joshua in on the monsters' present gambling game. Earlier, he'd howled over the Owl-in-his-underwear story.

"I was wondering," Joshua began, "if I could

borrow Taco for the weekend. My family is going to my cousins' farm, and Mom says we can take the dog with us—if it's okay with you."

"Sure," Rilla told him, wishing he'd ask *her* to go, too.

"Great," Joshua said. "I'll take good care of him."

Earth, you can't go away for the weekend, she reminded herself. *Who'd take care of the monsters?* "Have fun," she told him.

Setting the phone on the dresser, she climbed back into bed, trying not to upset Butterscotch's winning mountain of pennies.

The monsters were bickering at each other so loudly, Rilla wondered if she should turn on the radio to drown out their gibberish. Funny how quickly the shy one got over her need for peace and quiet.

Tap, tap, tap.

"Shhh!" Rilla held her breath to listen.

No one ever knocked on her door. Mr. Tamerow was in Helsinki and her father was in Oregon and Joshua just called to say he was leaving town, so who . . . ?

"Rill? It's me."

Sparrow?

"And Poppy. Can we come in?"

Rilla's heart went into hyperdrive. Mainly because she hadn't locked the door when she came in chatting on the phone with Joshua.

All Sparrow had to do was swing the door open and see the monsters. All three of them. Alive and feisty, quarreling on her bed.

"FREEZE!" she rasped.

Three pairs of monster eyes turned to gape at her.

"If you want to continue living here, stay completely and totally still. Do you understand?"

"But—" Owl began.

"Hush! This is real-l-l-l-ly important. Trust me. Pretend you're, you're *stuffed* monsters and you can't move at all."

Rilla waited to see if they'd react negatively to the idea of being stuffed, but they continued giving her a baffled stare.

Tap, tap, tap.

"I'll explain after they leave. Don't move the whole time they're here. Promise?" Rilla struggled to untangle herself from the quilt. "Owl, *please* make them understand."

Owl whisper-gibbered to the others, launching a heated discussion.

"Rilla? Are you in there?"

"Hush!" Rilla hissed at the monsters. Panic almost took her voice away. "In the name of granola and hot dogs and tasty literature—PLEASE SHUT UP AND DON'T MOVE!"

"Okey-dokey," chirped Owl.

Okey-dokey? What had he been eating now? Her slang dictionary?

Rilla positioned the monsters to make it look as if she'd set them there. "Remember," she whispered. "Stay frozen."

"Rilla Harmony Earth!"

"C-come in," she called, trying to keep her voice from shaking.

Sparrow shoved the door open in exasperation and stepped inside. Aunt Poppy was right behind her. "Must we know a secret password to enter your precious attic?"

Rilla thought she heard Owl snicker.

"Sorry. Um, guess I didn't hear you."

Aunt Poppy gestured toward her pajamas. "Are you in bed already? On a Friday night?"

Rilla shrugged. "I'm just reading." If she confessed to doing homework when she didn't have to, they'd probably call in Sparrow's psychic healer, Mother Lapis Lazuli—the *last* person Rilla wanted to deal with right now.

Sparrow perched on the desk chair and placed her fingers on the computer keyboard. "We want you to show us how to send e-mail."

Rilla was so nervous, her teeth began to chatter. "O-o-okey-dokey."

"Are you all right?" Aunt Poppy asked, pulling another chair up to the computer.

"I'm fine." Her voice sounded like a tiny bird peep. She glanced at the monsters. They were doing such a good job playing possum, she was tempted to offer words of encouragement.

"It takes a minute to connect to the Internet," Rilla said, thankful to hear her voice sounding almost normal.

Perhaps if she stood between the desk and the bed, no one would notice the monsters. After all, her bed was always piled high with stuffed animals—although they usually weren't gambling.

Rilla gave her mother and aunt a quick e-mail lesson. "Who are you writing to?" she asked. "Mr. Tamerow?"

"Yes," Sparrow answered. "And to David."

Rilla unintentionally reacted, making a tiny noise that sounded like one of Butter's whimper-whines.

Sparrow peered over the top of her glasses. "Do I need to ask your permission? I've known him longer than I've known you."

"No," Rilla said, correcting her. "You knew him first, but you've known me longer."

"Smart kid," Aunt Poppy said.

Sparrow began to type. She kept flubbing words and hitting the "Delete" key. "Oh, I can't do this. I'm too nervous. Sis, you do it."

The two traded places.

"Dear Abe," Aunt Poppy began, reading out loud as she typed. "Congratulations on your wonderful news. Harmony House can't wait to meet Minna and the twins."

Minna and the twins. Ugh. Sounded like one of José's former bands.

"Please join us with your new family to celebrate Christmas. And—ta-dah—to celebrate my holiday wedding to José."

Rilla showed Aunt Poppy how to send the message. In a cyber second, it was zipping its way to Helsinki.

"Amazing," Aunt Poppy whispered in awe. "Next letter," she began. "Dear David . . ."

Sparrow began to drum her fingers on the edge of the desk.

Rilla felt as uncomfortable as her mother. "Are you sure it's okay for him to come here?"

"Of course," Sparrow answered without hesitation. "Keeping you and your father apart was never my intention."

Rilla read the invitation over Aunt Poppy's shoulder as she typed it. *Whoa, this is really happening.*

"Done," Aunt Poppy said. "Think it'll work? Think he'll come?"

"If he's the same David I knew," Sparrow told her, "I think he'll be more than eager to meet his daughter."

Rilla zipped the message off to Oregon, then disconnected from the Internet.

The Earth sisters rose to leave.

"Thanks for letting us use your computer," Sparrow said. "But I prefer to stick with old-fashioned letter writing."

Rilla held her breath. *I can't believe they're actually leaving the attic without noticing—!*

"Ooooh," squealed Aunt Poppy, pointing at the bed. "Look! It's Rilla's monsters!"

28

Monster Moment of Truth

Omigosh, omigosh, omigosh.

Rilla prayed the monsters would *not* react.

Stay frozen, stay frozen, stay frozen.

Aunt Poppy hurried to the bed to examine Owl—the one Rilla hadn't shown anyone. How could she? He'd arrived alive.

"Is this one new?" Aunt Poppy asked. "Don't think I've seen him before."

"He's the Sep-Sep-September monster," Rilla stammered.

Sparrow and Aunt Poppy studied the incredibly odd scene on the bed, then exchanged worried glances.

"So, what are you doing here?" Sparrow asked. "Playing a game? With your stuffed toys?" She gave Rilla her "How old *are* you?" look.

"Oh, gosh." Rilla waved a hand over the bed in an attempt to diminish the weirdness of the situation. "Just fooling around. Seeing if I could get the, um, toys to stay propped up like they were, um, playing a game."

Please don't touch any of them, Rilla pleaded silently.

Aunt Poppy whisked Owl off the bed.

Rilla went numb. If Owl suddenly thrust out a paw and gave Aunt Poppy a piece of his monster mind . . . well, it could be heart attack city.

Owl stayed frozen! What a prince. He even kept his legs bent in a sitting position when Aunt Poppy held him high like a newborn, then clutched him in a suffocating hug.

Rilla heard a definite grunt along with the hug. She held her breath.

Aunt Poppy laughed.

Rilla gaped at her. Owl had just made a noise! Why the laugh?

"Cute, cute, cute." Aunt Poppy held him out to Sparrow. "This one's got one of those noise thingies inside that does sound effects."

Noise thingies? *Geez.*

Sparrow straightened Sparkler's vest, then reached for the peace symbol around Butterscotch's neck.

NO!

Rilla stayed as motionless as the monsters. No way would Butter let Sparrow remove the peace symbol.

STAY STILL! she shouted—from her brain to the monster's—or whatever was inside Butterscotch's head.

"Look," Sparrow said. "This one's eyes follow my hand." Leaving the leather strap around Butterscotch's neck, Sparrow moved the symbol back and forth a few times. The monster's suspicious gaze followed each move.

STOP IT! Rilla felt choked, like she was drowning. One tiny move and her monster secret would be out in the open. Might as well e-mail the *National Enquirer* right now and say, "Come on over! Have we got a blockbuster story for you!"

Sparrow dropped the peace symbol into Butterscotch's lap and faced Rilla. "That belonged to your father, didn't it?"

Rilla nodded, unsure of her voice.

"Why did you . . . ?"

Rilla shrugged, kicking at the bedpost, like it was no big deal. "Butterscotch wanted to wear it. So I let her." *Ha, ha, ha.*

Sparrow and Aunt Poppy contemplated her answer.

"I was joking," she told them.

They didn't laugh.

Aunt Poppy tossed Owl onto the bed. He rolled onto his side, paws extended, and stayed in that position. Rilla loved him for it.

"Hey, kid," her aunt began. "José and I are going downtown to the fall street carnival. Why don't you come with us?"

Sparrow moved toward Rilla, looking concerned. "Good idea, Rill. You need to get out of here and do something fun. After all, it *is* Friday night."

What Rilla *needed* was for them to leave. "I really don't want to go."

More exchanged glances.

R-i-i-i-ng-g-g-g!

All three monsters flinched at the ringing phone. Luckily, no one noticed except her.

Aunt Poppy reached for the phone Rilla had left on the dresser.

"Hello?" A smug grin settled onto her face. "For you," she said, handing the phone to Rilla.

"Hello?"

"Hel-l-l-l-oooo."

Andrew? Calling on Friday night? Nifty.

Rilla waved her mother and aunt toward the door. The only thing worse than having them pop into her attic was having them listen in on a phone conversation between her and a boy.

They stayed no matter how hard she flapped her arm.

"I'm calling," Andrew began, "because my parents and I are going downtown for the fall street carnival, and I was, um, wondering if you could go with us—I mean, go with me. We have to *ride* with them, but once we get downtown, we can do the booths by ourselves, and—"

"Okay," Rilla blurted. He didn't need to explain any further. "The carnival sounds like fun."

She tried not to giggle in his ear. What *was* she doing climbing into bed on a Friday night to do homework? *Get a grip, Earth.*

"You can go?" Andrew sounded relieved and pleased at the same time. "Can you be ready in a half hour?"

"Sure."

"Great! See ya."

Rilla shut off the phone and handed it to her mother to carry back to the third-floor landing. "Now, if you ladies will excuse me," she snipped playfully, "I have a date to get ready for."

Worry faded from Sparrow's face.

"La-de-dah," teased Aunt Poppy. "I guess José and I are second choice." She mussed Rilla's hair. "See you downtown, kid."

Sparrow gave the monsters one last puzzled glance, then followed Aunt Poppy down the steps. "My little girl is growing up," Rilla heard her say.

"Heaven help us," answered Aunt Poppy.

Then the Earth sisters laughed.

29

More Magic on the Way

"Thank you, thank you, thank you," Rilla gushed to her monster allies. "You guys were great! Real actors."

The monsters remained frozen. Owl on his side. Sparkler a bit cockeyed. Butter with a crabby expression on her face, and one paw clutching her precious peace symbol.

"You can move now," Rilla told them.

No reaction.

"Oh, no!" Rilla's cry stuck in her throat.

Could the magic have broken that fast? Could the monsters have returned to their stuffed and silent state all at once? Just like that?

But she wasn't ready for it to happen. She wasn't ready to let them go.

Don't cry; you've got to look nice for Andrew.

Slumping onto the bed, Rilla put her head in her hands. How could they leave her?

A fuzzy paw touched her leg.

Rilla's head jerked up.

Three monsters smirked at her. Mischief twinkled in their eyes.

"Fooled ya," Owl teased.

Rilla collapsed onto the bed.

The monsters jumped on top of her. She hugged them—but not for long. Monsters were worse than cats when it came to hugging.

Sparkler leaped off the bed, grabbed his skateboard, and headed for the shuffleboard mat.

Owl climbed onto the bookshelf to nibble a magazine.

"Come," Rilla said to Butterscotch. "You can help me get ready for my date." Taking her paw, she led the monster into the bathroom.

Rilla pulled the cosmetic sampler from the cabinet. "How would you like to polish your claws after I paint my fingernails?"

The suggestion clearly thrilled Butterscotch. Climbing onto the towel hamper, she handed Rilla a brush and comb, blusher and lip gloss, then settled in to watch the MonsterMom get ready for her date.

After she primped in front of the mirror, Rilla put on her best jeans and sweater and began to hum a Christmas song. Boy, she had a lot to look forward to in the next few months:

The wedding.

The holidays.

Meeting her father. (Big gulp.)

Then, of course, three more monsters were due to arrive before the end of the year. Ho, boy. More magic on the way.

But right now she had equally important things to worry about—like which shade of nail polish to choose.

Sometimes life could be soooo complicated. It would be nice to have a little help making important decisions.

So she let Butter choose a shade of polish for her.

Poppy Harmony Earth
and
José Pablo Pacheco

request the honor of your presence
at the celebration of their wedding
Christmas Eve
One o'clock
Harmony House Parlor

Reception immediately following ceremony

In lieu of wedding gifts,
donations may be made to
Save the Earth, Inc.